My Forever

Arbor Falls Book 4

MAYA NICOLE

Copyright 2021 © Maya Nicole
All rights reserved.

No portion of this book may be reproduced in any form without permission from the author, except as permitted by U.S. copyright law.

For permissions contact: mayanicoleauthor@gmail.com

This book is currently available exclusively through Amazon.

The characters and events portrayed in this book are fictitious. Any similarity to real people, living or dead, businesses, or locales are coincidental.

Cover Design by Mayflower Studio

Edited by Karen Sanders Editing
Proofreading by Proofs by Polly

❦ Created with Vellum

AUTHOR'S NOTE

Arbor Falls is a reverse harem romance series. That means the main character will have a happily ever after with three or more men. Recommended for readers 18+ for adult content and language.

This book is dedicated to surviving cliffhangers.

CHAPTER ONE

Ivy

There are moments in life that define us. For some, it's a marriage or buying their dream home. For others, it's the birth of a child. For me? It was Cole coming into my life.

I'd never given a lot of thought about my future, instead, focusing on the here and now. With him... with all of them, I saw my future laid out before me. There'd be highs and lows, but together we'd make it through the worst.

But that wasn't my defining moment.

The arrow came out of nowhere, catching the light in such a way that made it appear to be a ray of sunlight sent from heaven.

Or it was sent from hell.

A split-second decision. A defining moment.

There was a second of silence, then chaos erupted.

He didn't shoot again, but he was still there watching. Waiting.

It seemed like a lifetime, but wasn't more than thirty seconds before most of the pack dispersed, some frantic and others staying calm. Those that remained were high-ranking wolves, betas, and trainees. They looked at me for direction.

"I've got him." Eli helped lay Cole back onto the deck. "Go catch that motherfucker."

Silas's eyes met mine, and he nodded. We both jumped from the deck, shifting midair and hitting the ground running, our other pack members behind us.

I was mentally strategizing taking out the threat, but we needed some wolves to guard the house too. *"Rover, stay behind with your team and make sure they're safe."* Five wolves split from us, fanning around the yard.

There was always the possibility that there was more than one shooter, but with a dozen wolves running straight for him, he'd have been stupid to stay. As we neared his position, he hesitated for a moment before he turned and ran.

But not before I caught a glimpse of his face. The same face from the visions I'd had in the pool of insight.

Apollo.

"He's here to kill me. I'm not sure we can kill him, but we can chase him away." I felt the agreement of my pack members through our connection. *"Manny, take your*

team and head to the right. Silas head to the left with yours. The rest of us will keep chasing him."

No one argued with my decision, and we split into three groups. Apollo was fast, but he seemed to be holding back his speed. He occasionally looked over his shoulder, a smirk on his face and his golden eyes twinkling like he was having a splendid time.

If we caught him, I'd show him a splendid time when I shoved his bow straight up his ass.

This was my *uncle*, and he was trying to kill me. Would the wrath of the gods really rain down on Artemis for falling in love and having a child?

Sounded ludicrous to me.

From what Trevor had told us, Apollo was out of stasis more often than Artemis was and ran the entire coalition operation. He wasn't doing that great of a job if he somehow let it slip his notice that a lunatic had been working for him.

We were gaining on him, and he turned and ran backward, practically floating through the air. Quicker than I'd seen anyone move, he lifted his bow and shot right at me. I jumped out of the way just in time to avoid the arrow.

I didn't exactly know what we were going to do if we did catch up to him. I doubted a pack of wolves could take down a god. But I was half god, so where did that put me?

"Where the hell is he going?" Rory, one of the new beta trainees, was keeping up with the other wolves just fine. There had been some doubts at first when I'd

suggested taking on a few women to train in the traditionally male-led role.

Wolves had pushed back, and still did from time to time, but for the most part, things were going well with the small changes I'd made to be more inclusive.

We were almost to the clearing, which was one of my favorite places. My deer friends visited me often when I was there, and surprisingly, my appetite for them had all but vanished.

Cole said it was probably because my mother was the goddess of nature and killing them was against my instinct. If that were the case, wouldn't I be vegetarian or vegan?

Apollo turned around again, just as we exited the trees. He nocked his arrow, but then he was sent crashing to the ground as a large gray wolf barreled into him like a freight train.

One second they were a tangle of man and beast, the next, they were gone.

I skidded to a stop where they had just been and looked around frantically. *"Where did they go? Silas? Where are you?"*

His connection wasn't there. He was completely cut off from me.

I sniffed the ground and air frantically. I could smell right where they had been. They had vanished into thin air. How?

"Alpha, come look at this." Manny was standing not far away, and I ran to him, looking down at what he was staring at.

"What the hell is this?" There was a symbol in the

shape of a harp on the ground, and it was glowing gold, just like the arrow that had pierced Cole's chest.

I was certain it hadn't been there before because I'd run and rolled around in just about every square inch of the field, marking it with my scent.

As we stood over the symbol, it slowly disappeared, leaving nothing behind but our confusion. Manny reached forward with his paw and jumped back, shaking it. *"Son of a bitch! It burned me!"*

Well, I certainly wasn't going to touch it then.

"How could they just disappear?" I turned around in a circle, trying to figure out where they had gone. *"Do portals exist? I mean, they probably do since we exist."*

"Ivy, we need you back at the house." Eli's voice was laced with worry, and my stomach turned. If anything happened to Cole...

I couldn't think about it. He had to be okay. We'd been through so much already, and losing him would rip a piece of my soul away.

"We're on our way."

I didn't want to tell him that Silas had been taken. That could wait. There wasn't much that could be done besides go back to the house and call Trevor. He should have warned us Apollo was awake. How would Apollo have even known about me still being alive?

"Rory and Owen, come back to the house with me. The rest of you, scour this clearing and surrounding forest for any signs of Silas. Notify me immediately if he turns up or if you catch his scent."

I ran back to the house faster than I'd ever run

before. My lungs and limbs were burning by the time I leapt onto the deck and shifted back.

There was a small puddle of blood where Cole had fallen and droplets leading into the house. If Apollo's purpose were to kill me, he would have aimed for my heart, which meant the arrow most likely hit Cole just below his. I didn't know what was in that area, but it couldn't be good.

I rushed inside, a sense of dread filling me. Even when Cole had been shot by Dante, I knew deep down he would be okay. Sure, I'd been scared, but it hadn't felt like this. Like death was in the air.

I made it as far as the living room when I heard small inhales of breath coming from the couch. Xander was in a fetal position with his arms wrapped around his legs. He hadn't shifted, which was a relief. It was an ongoing worry of all of ours that if something bad happened, and he shifted again, he might not come back from it.

"Hey, I'm here." I walked around the couch and squatted in front of him, placing my hand on his cheek. "I'm safe. You're safe."

He squeezed his eyes shut and nodded. There was only so much the human mind could take before it shut down. If I lost Cole, I'd be losing Xander too.

The thought nearly knocked me on my ass, and I bit my inner cheek, the copper taste of my blood hitting my tongue. I needed to stay strong, but I wanted to scream.

"I'm going down to the basement now to heal Cole. Are you going to be all right by yourself or do you want me to have Rory and Owen come in and sit with you?"

"I'm fine." His voice was hoarse and barely audible, but he'd spoken, which made me sigh in relief.

Quickly brushing my lips across his, I squeezed his arm and started toward the hallway.

"Ivy?" Xander sat up, his darkened green eyes wrecking me with the fear in them. "Where's Silas? Can he come sit with me?"

"He's securing the perimeter with the betas." The lie burned like acid on my tongue, but I couldn't tell him the truth and send him into a bigger spiral than he was already in. "Call for me if you need me."

Hurt washed across his features, and he nodded before lying back down, the tiniest whimper coming from him.

He knew.

He had to. Eli probably did too. I could feel that Silas wasn't near, and I was sure if either of them tried to speak to him, they'd find an empty void where his connection should have been.

I walked calmly to the basement door, but as soon as my feet hit the stairs, I ran down them as fast as I could. Grabbing a pair of shorts and a t-shirt from the cabinet, I slowly opened the medical room door, not sure what I'd find on the other side.

Eli and Sara were there, but a few other pack members were assisting.

Shit. The only people who knew about my healing abilities were my mates, Sara, and Manny. The last thing we needed was for the pack to know that I was special in a different way.

I didn't think they would care, since most had taken well to me being in charge. But I could foresee constantly being called for every little ailment.

"How is he?" I pulled on my clothes and stood next to the exam table.

I'd become a lot less squeamish around blood, but seeing Cole's chest cut open made me feel lightheaded. Looking away, I shut my eyes briefly to calm myself down. The arrow was piercing a lung, blood and bubbles coming out with every rattling breath he took.

"We didn't want to take the arrow out until you got here. Should we have Ava and Ben step out?" Sara didn't look up from what she was doing. "There are too many people in here, anyway."

Ava and Ben looked at me for direction. "Why don't you two go upstairs and make sure Xander is all right." They nodded somberly and headed out of the room.

Eli quickly shut the door and locked it. "We can't touch the arrow."

"What do you mean you can't touch it?" I looked closer at it and it looked like a standard arrow besides the fact that it was gold. "Is it lodged in the bone or something?"

I didn't know the first thing about medical procedures or human anatomy. Eli and Sara weren't really equipped to deal with this kind of injury, but with wolf healing, usually everything was fine. What the pack really needed was a doctor, or at the very least a veterinarian.

"It burned me when I tried to snap part of it off to make it easier to work around." Eli held out his hand and there was a welt in the middle of his palm.

I immediately reached for it, and he hissed in a breath as my glowing thumb glided over it. Nothing happened.

"Why the hell isn't it healing?" I pulled my hand away and tried my other one. Still nothing. "It was Apollo who shot the arrow. Do you think that has anything to do with it?"

"Like, the actual Apollo? Greek god Apollo?" Sara's mouth hung open as she stood across from us on the other side of the table.

Talking about the gods was one thing, but knowing they physically existed and came around was another. I'd seen him with my own eyes in the pool of insight and now in the flesh.

"That's the one." I looked down at Cole before touching the end with my finger. When my finger didn't burn, I pinched the end carefully between two fingers. "It's letting me touch it. I'll remove it."

"Go scrub your hands in the sink. We need to take more precautions since we don't know what we're dealing with." Sara was setting up a tray with instruments and paused to look up at me. "If you can't heal Eli's hand, there's the possibility you won't be able to heal Cole."

Fear twisted in my belly, and I walked to the sink. Turning on the water to hot, a million scenarios played out in my head, but one possibility nearly sent me to my knees; Cole could die.

After scrubbing like I was going into surgery, I dried my hands and walked to the table with my arms held up in front of me like a surgeon.

The corners of Eli's lips twitched, and he shook his head. "This isn't *Grey's Anatomy*."

"Let's get this arrow out. What do I do? Just grab and pull?" I reached forward to grab it and Sara blocked my hand.

"No. We'll tell you when to pull it out nice and slow. We need to cut his lung so the arrowhead slides out. We would push it through, but its trajectory is leading to his spine. He got lucky it didn't go farther."

I looked away as they started cutting. The last thing we needed was for me to pass out, and cutting into a lung might just do that. It felt wrong to be operating on Cole, but there wasn't another choice. It would have taken too long for a doctor to get there.

How could a pack have over four hundred people and have only one doctor that mostly worked with humans? With everything going on, we needed to reassess how readily available the doctor was.

"Okay, Ivy. Slowly pull it out. Straight up," Eli said.

Taking a deep breath, I wrapped my hand around the arrow and slowly pulled up. Sara and Eli helped guide us out of the hole. I set it down on the tray and let out the breath I'd been holding.

"Try to heal him." Sara lifted the gauze off the wound, and I put my hand over it, feeling my hands heat up and it transferring to him.

"It's not working." Eli gently pushed me out of the way and he and Sara began working to patch up Cole.

"Ivy. Go check to see where the doctor is and call Trevor. He might know something about that arrow."

"What about shifting? Can you get him to shift?" Probably shifting with an open wound wasn't the best, but if we healed faster in our wolf forms, it might help.

"He has no control over whether or not he can shift right now. Plus, this arrow is not a normal one." Eli shook his head. "Let us patch him up, and I'll call you back down here to try to heal him again once we've repaired some of the damage."

I left the room, knowing I needed to give them space to focus on fixing Cole. I trusted Eli and Sara to do what was best for him, but I was still unsure if we were taking the right approach. A hospital might have been a better solution.

But that wasn't a possibility.

I walked upstairs to find the living room empty. Ava was standing at the sliding glass door, peering out.

"What's going on? Where's Xander?"

"He's out in Silas's workshop. Rory, Owen, and Ben are making sure he doesn't leave. How's Cole?" She looked at me and twisted her lips to the side. "And why is someone trying to kill you with an arrow?"

"It's complicated." Eventually, I would have to explain things to the pack. If I wanted to continue making progress as alpha, they needed to trust that I was telling them important information. "Cole is..."

My eyes swam with tears, and she put her hand on my shoulder. "He'll pull through."

I sure hoped so.

I walked out the door and the short distance to

Silas's workshop. Xander had been spending a lot of time with Silas over the last few weeks, watching as he did his art.

Opening the door, I peeked inside. Xander was sitting on the loveseat, staring at the sheet thrown over the sculpture Silas was making for me. I still had no idea what he was making, and he refused to let me look.

"Is Cole okay?" He didn't turn to look at me, remaining still on the loveseat that had been moved to the middle of the room.

"He'll be fine." I couldn't keep the worry out of my voice, and he turned his head. "He'll be fine."

The tears falling down my cheeks didn't hide my true feelings. His face softened, and he patted the loveseat next to him. I quickly went to him and fell into his arms. I should have been the one giving him comfort, not the other way around.

"Is he going to die?" Xander's lips were against my hair, and I shuddered at the thought of losing Cole.

"It's not looking good."

And it was all my fault.

CHAPTER TWO

Xander

The urge to retreat into my wolf was strong. From the second the arrow flew through the air to now, it had taken everything within me not to give into my wolf and shift. My wolf was in bad shape and coming back would be difficult.

I might not come back at all.

There were plenty of shifters that had been known to be taken over by their wolves. But no one ever really talked about what happened to them in the end.

My guess was they were no longer alive.

I shut my eyes as I rested the side of my face against Ivy's hair. If Cole died, it would change everything. Over the past several weeks, we'd all grown closer and started to heal.

We were an actual family unit now. There were

occasionally still scuffles, but for the most part, we had reached a blissful state of happiness.

"This is all because of me. If I wouldn't have shown up here, none of this would be happening. The OQ wouldn't have found the pack, the coalition wouldn't have gotten involved, Apollo wouldn't even know you existed." I let a few of my own tears fall, knowing that if I kept them bottled up, they'd eat me alive.

Ivy pulled away from me and gave me an incredulous look. "Don't you dare start that again, Xander. None of this is your fault. Everything that has happened, has been for a reason, don't you sense that? I need you like I need the others." She cupped my face, and I leaned into her touch. "Please tell me you know that I need you."

"How can you need somebody so broken? What do I have to offer you besides more pain and more worry?" My voice cracked, and I suppressed the urge to sob like a fucking baby. I'd done enough of that.

"We're all broken. I need your love, I need your humor, and I definitely need your dancing." A soft smile played at her lips as she stroked her thumbs to clear away my tears. "This will eventually all be over, and we will all have our happily ever after."

I nodded and leaned back against the back of the couch, taking her with me. "Where's Silas?" I'd already tried to reach out to him and was met with silence. Even with Cole, there was at least a little bit of a connection, despite him being injured.

"He's patrolling." I could tell she was lying, and I put

my hands on hers. "Let's just worry about keeping you here with us."

"You're lying. I need to know."

She bit her lip and more tears fell down her cheeks. "He attacked Apollo, and then they vanished. They were rolling around in the dirt one minute, and the next, they were gone."

"Fuck." I jumped off the couch and looked down at her. "You should have said something. We could be out there looking for him." My wolf was pushing to the surface, which she could probably see because she stood quickly and took my hands.

"Don't, Xander. I have people looking for him and patrolling to see if there are any signs of him. I need to call Trevor and find out if he knows where Apollo is and about this arrow he used."

I took deep breaths and focused on her gray eyes, which were almost glowing silver. They only glowed like that when she was angry or using a power that wasn't from her wolf. That was the theory anyway.

"Why don't you tell me about what he's working on for me." She walked over to the sculpture and ran a finger over the sheet covering it. "Do you think he'll get mad if I have a little peek?"

She started to lift the sheet, and I grabbed her around the waist and led her back to the loveseat, pulling her down onto my lap.

"Don't you dare." I buried my face in the crook of her neck. "I've been sworn to secrecy, and if he finds out you've seen it, things are going to get ugly."

I loved how quickly she could pull me out of my

own head. My wolf was already relaxing, and I felt myself getting farther and farther away from that place that made me want to just leave myself.

"Come with me and we'll call Trevor together." She wiggled out of my lap and held out her hand. "You shouldn't be alone right now. None of us should."

∼

Our conversation with Trevor had been short, but he confirmed that Apollo was indeed awake but hadn't been for long. He seemed worried about Apollo taking Silas, which put me and Ivy even more on edge. He said he'd have to call us back.

It had been two hours since we made the call and almost two and a half since Cole had been shot. Eli and Sara were still working on repairing the damage that had been done to Cole. Ivy had checked in a few times, but they said every time they'd tried to close his wound, it would open back up. Ivy had tried two more times to heal him with no result.

I was just about to fall asleep with my head on Ivy's shoulder when the basement door opened and Eli's grunting grabbed my attention. Ivy and I both jumped off the couch at the same time and rushed to help him. He was carrying Cole; his abdomen was wrapped.

"What are you doing?" Ivy followed quickly behind Eli as he started to move up the stairs. "Were you able to get his wound closed?"

Eli shook his head, not saying a word as we made

our way up the stairs into the bedroom. I didn't like that he was so quiet. And neither did my wolf.

Sara came up behind us and laid a clean sheet on the bed before Eli put him down. "We had to leave the wound open because it wouldn't heal. Any word from Trevor?"

"No. What do you mean it's not healing? I should try again." Ivy crawled across the bed to the other side of Cole.

"It's not going to work, Ivy. There's something about that arrow that counteracts our wolves' healing ability and yours." Eli pulled a second sheet over Cole. "I'm going to go call his dad."

An intense feeling of loss coursed through my body, and I backed against the wall, shaking my head.

No. We couldn't lose Cole.

Eli came to a stop in front of me and gently touched my arm. "Hey, stay with us. Go be with them while I make the call."

I nodded, and he quickly brushed his lips over mine before leaving the bedroom, shutting the door behind him.

Crawling across the large bed, I settled next to Ivy, who was lying right against Cole with one of her legs over his. I wrapped an arm around her and buried my face in her hair.

Everything would be okay. It had to be.

~

I MUST HAVE FALLEN asleep because a short time later I jolted awake to the sounds of hushed arguing in the hall. Ivy was conked out, her hand resting over Cole's wound, glowing faintly. I didn't think it was doing anything, though.

Cole's face was devoid of color, and his breaths were rattling in his chest. If he wasn't a wolf, I would have said he was on his deathbed.

I carefully climbed out of bed and slipped out of the room, finding Eli and Sara in a heated argument in the hallway.

"What's going on?" I approached with caution because Sara had a glint in her eye that said she was getting ready to punch her brother in the arm.

"Eli thinks we should remove his lung because any tissue that was touched by the arrow isn't healing. I told him I don't think we're to that point yet. He'll never be the same if we take his lung." Sara's voice was rising with every word.

"Keep your voices down." I looked over my shoulder at the door. I didn't want Ivy to hear. "Are you two even equipped to do that? What if it doesn't work?"

"It's not that difficult. Once we remove it, we can sew up everything or Ivy can heal him. The doctor that services our pack and Tahoe won't be here for another hour. I don't think we have an hour." Eli crossed his arms over his chest. "I tried Trevor again, and he's not answering his cell phone. The only other choice we have is to take him to the hospital, and then what? He'll expose us all." Eli was screaming in a whisper.

I put my hand on his arm, hoping he'd calm down.

"He'll be okay for now, right? What difference does it make if we leave him as he is right now or if you take out his lung and whatever else you need to?"

"Right now, his body is spending all of its resources trying to heal, but it's just going to waste. He's going to run out of energy and then we'll lose him. By removing what won't heal, we have a fighting chance. He can live without a lung." His logic made sense, but taking out a lung seemed drastic. Even then, there was the issue of what the arrow touched going in.

"What did his dad say?"

"They're in Michigan and will be here as soon as they can. I sent the helicopter to get them, but it still will take them a while. He said to do what I needed to do to keep him alive." Eli pinched the bridge of his nose. "Removing his lung will keep him alive."

Sara threw her hands up in the air. "He's alive right now. We're not going to go chopping out his body parts because you think that might help. We put in a call for help to the coalition and for the doctor. We have time."

Without another word, she went back into the bedroom and shut the door behind her. Eli let out a frustrated growl and began pacing the hallway, his hands in his hair.

"I'll make you some food and then we can lie down for a while. I'm a little hungry myself." I wanted to hold him, but he looked like if I touched him he'd snap. "Or since you're the better cook, you can make me some food."

"I'm not hungry or tired." He stopped pacing and

stared at the bedroom door. "Where's Silas?"

"Apollo took him." I flinched as he turned and stared at me, his eyes blinking rapidly. "Vanished into thin air."

Eli's hands clenched at his sides, and he shut his eyes. "Are we ever just going to be able to breathe again?" His voice raised at the end, slightly hysterical.

"Let's go get some food. Ivy will call us if we're needed. She and your sister could probably use something to eat too." I approached him carefully and put my arm around his shoulders, leading him away from the bedroom and to the stairs.

Once we were downstairs and in the kitchen, Eli relaxed a little and pulled ingredients out of the refrigerator and pantry. I sat at the island and watched him work as he made sandwiches for us.

I had so many things I wanted to say to him but didn't know how to say them or if it was the right time. Instead, I rested my cheek in my hand as he moved around the kitchen. The kitchen was his safe place and therefore, was mine as well. Wherever he or Ivy were, that was where I let everything else fall away.

Hell, even Silas and Cole had become tethers holding me in place over the last few weeks. Silas was soothing to watch as he used his hands to create something magnificent. Cole was someone I could talk to about music and cars for hours with. I never thought I'd find two best friends in them, but I had.

"What are you thinking about?" Eli set a plate in front of me and went to the refrigerator, pulling out two Cokes and sitting down next to me.

"Just how much I love all of you." I picked up my sandwich and looked over to find him staring at me. "What?"

"I love you."

A lump rose in my throat and I put my sandwich down, turning toward him. "Tell me again."

"I love you, Xan." His hand gripped the back of my neck, pulling me toward him so our foreheads were touching. "Don't leave me."

Fuck.

"I'm not going anywhere." I held onto his arm, my vision blurring. "I love you."

We sat like that for a few minutes before Eli cleared his throat and started to pull away. I leaned in for a kiss, capturing his lips with mine. Kissing him made everything else fade into the background.

When we finally pulled apart, his cheeks were flushed, and I couldn't stop a smile from escaping. "Let's eat."

"Eat?" His eyes fell to my lips. "You're beautiful when you smile."

"Beautiful?" My smile widened. "I prefer handsome or sexy. Charming would work too."

He rolled his eyes and turned toward his food. "You know what I mean."

I put my hand on his thigh as we ate in silence. I didn't know what the hell was going to happen in the next several hours or days, but what I did know was I was loved, and sometimes that's all you need to get through the storm.

CHAPTER THREE

Silas

I woke up to the clanging of metal on metal.

All I could remember was jumping on Apollo and then nothing. Attacking a god probably wasn't the best decision in the world.

At least I still had my head.

The clanging was driving me up a wall, and I opened my eyes, looking around the jail cell I was in. Everything was metal and concrete, built to withstand the strength of a shifter.

For a moment, my heart beat uncontrollably, remembering what had happened the last time I'd been locked up.

This isn't the OQ, Silas. Breathe.

Shaking my head, I stood and stretched, my entire body protesting the movement after sleeping on a hard metal surface for who knew how long. I could see all the cells across from mine, each with a man inside. They all appeared to be sleeping.

Oh, well.

"Hey!" The man directly across from me bolted upright from his bed—if it could even be called that. "Where the fuck are we?"

The man laughed, the sound echoing in the space devoid of anything to absorb the noise. "Azkaban." He laid back down with a grunt.

"Aska what?" I walked to the bars, grabbing onto them.

"You fucked up, man. You're in prison." The man one cell over from the smartass was at the bars of his cell. "They usually have a trial pretty quickly after you've been brought in to decide if you should rot away in here, be released, or die."

"But I didn't do anything!" Except attack a Greek god. "Don't I get a phone call or a lawyer?"

The man laughed so hard he started coughing. These men were of no use to me, so I sat down at the small table that had a single chair bolted to the floor. Someone would be by eventually.

Eventually turned into what felt like days. I was nodding off again when the sound of heels came from down the hall and nearly every fucker in the place started shouting obscenities and clanging metal cups against the bars.

Jumping up, I joined them—minus the shouting—sticking my face against the bars, trying to see who was coming. There were two sets of footsteps, one a woman's and the other probably a man's. But what did I know? Men wore heeled shoes now.

My eyes widened as they came into view. I didn't know the man, but the woman had even brighter red hair than Ivy. Was this the fox shifter we'd learned about?

"Silas Simmons?" Well, shit. She even sounded like Ivy. Were they related? Had Artemis just gone around getting pregnant by all the different types of shifters there might be?

"Over here, baby." The man in the cell across from me was right at the bars, his hands reaching through, trying to grasp at nothing but air. "I knew you'd come for me."

The guard smacked his arms with a club he was carrying, and the man yelped, moving away from the bars, holding his arm.

"I'm Silas." I stood back so I wouldn't get hit with anything. "I think there's been a mistake. I haven't committed any crime."

"That's what everyone says. At least you put on pants." Her lip curled in disgust. "Turn around and put your arms out."

I did as she asked, and the man unlocked my cell and cuffed my hands behind my back. I'd never been in handcuffs before, and I couldn't say I enjoyed the torque in my shoulders and upper back. But I was also getting old.

The guard took my upper arm in a vice grip as we followed the woman back down the hall. The taunts from the prisoners ranged from threats of sexual violence to death. I didn't belong in a place with such heathens. It was a place for the depraved, not an upstanding man like me who sculpted phallic art for a living.

We went out a door, down a hall, and through another door to what looked a lot like the coalition's headquarters. There hadn't been a word spoken about there being a prison or jail on site the few times we'd been there.

The woman opened a door and gestured for me to enter. It was a standard interrogation room, like you might see in a police station. I sat in the chair that was secured to the floor.

"Can someone tell me what the hell is going on? Last time I checked, tackling someone wasn't against any kind of law." It probably was an assault, but in the shifter world, we didn't abide by human laws when we were in our own territories.

The guard pushed a button and cuffs popped up from the table. He uncuffed me. "Put your hands on the table."

"Look man, I think you're attractive, but I'm not really into being cuffed." I smirked and then flinched as he grabbed my arm and slammed it down so my wrist was in the cuff. "That was a little unnecessary, don't you think?"

I put my other arm on the table without his help and glared at him. He must have had nerves of steel because his face was indifferent as he closed the cuffs. He looked like he could snap me in two if I got out of line.

My attention went back to the doorway where the woman was standing with her arms crossed. "You look like my girlfriend."

"Mr. Simmons, you're not helping your case any. You attacked one of our top agents." Top agents? So, not everyone knew Apollo existed. Interesting. "You're facing twenty years."

"Twenty years?" I tried to jump up but was locked in place. "He tried to kill my girlfriend and instead, my best friend was shot!"

Confusion crossed her features, and she shifted from one foot to the other. What the hell had he told them? "It's not up to me to decide if you're guilty."

Before I could give her a bigger piece of my mind, they both walked out, shutting the door behind them. How could I be facing prison when all I did was tackle the son of a bitch?

The time passed slowly, and I was just about ready to start yelling when the door opened and my father walked in. He looked back over his shoulder and then shut the door, quickly making his way to the table and sitting across from me.

"What have you done?" He reached across and took my hands. "I get out of a meeting, and I'm told my son is locked up for attacking an agent."

"That *agent* shot a fucking arrow at Ivy, and now Cole has a fucking arrow sticking out of his chest." He didn't react. "You knew that though, didn't you?"

"Ivy called." He released my hands and sat back in his chair. "I don't know where the *agent* went after he dropped you off here."

"Well, that's convenient. Who's the redhead chick? Artemis just dumps her baby and then goes and fucks another man?"

The viewing window, that I hadn't even paid any attention to, burst, sending glass flying everywhere. I slammed my eyes shut as it rained down on us, but that was short-lived because a fist hit me right in the center of my face.

My head snapped back, the sound of the bones in my nose crunching making me want to puke. I blacked out for a second and came to with a shirt held against my nose.

"You're being irrational. You can't just go around shooting innocent people or drawing attention to yourself by arresting someone for no reason." My dad was angry, and all I could smell was his scent. My vision was swimming, but I was fairly certain his shirt was pressed against my face.

"We had an arrangement, Trevor." The man who had punched the shit out of my face was pacing on the other side of the room. His voice was silky and immediately put me on edge. "As per our agreement, Silas is now mine."

"He's a grown man." He sounded resigned to my fate. Some fucking father he was.

My hands had been freed, and I took over holding the shirt. "Fuck you." The words came out muffled, but I was sure Apollo understood because he stopped pacing and stared at me. I removed the shirt so I could speak clearly. "I don't give a fuck who you are. I belong to no one, and if you think you're going to kill my mate, you're sorely mistaken."

"Is this the kind of insubordination you've been teaching the wolves?" Apollo put his hands on his hips and glared at my father. "You don't understand what is at stake here."

"You're right. I don't. So, please, tell us why you want her dead." My father crossed his arms over his naked chest. That was more like it. If we teamed up, maybe we could take the god out.

"You would do anything to protect your child, correct?" Apollo put his hands on the table and leaned on it. "Well, I'll do anything to protect my sister. Her indiscretions with that alpha have consequences."

"What about her other daughter? The one that brought me in here? She works here. Why aren't you off trying to kill her?" I wiped my nose, blood still coming from it even though it was healing.

Apollo stared at me like I had ten heads. "Artemis has one child."

"Then who-"

My father's hand clamped down on my shoulder. "We need to know how to counteract the arrow you shot. The wound isn't healing."

What did he mean, it wasn't healing? Ivy should have easily been able to heal Cole. The arrow hadn't hit his heart. At least it hadn't looked like it from where I'd been standing.

"There's no healing from a gilded arrow." Apollo sat down in the chair across from me and crossed his legs on top of the table. He was a cocky son of a bitch, and I wanted to wipe the smug expression off his face. "How about we make a deal?"

My dad sighed, and I looked up at him in disbelief. He couldn't really be entertaining this asshole, could he?

"What's your deal?"

The brightest grin I'd ever seen spread across Apollo's face. "I want Ivy—dead or alive is acceptable—and I'll heal the man I hit and let Silas go. I'd prefer not to go obtain her myself. It really puts a damper on my day."

"Deal."

"You son of a bitch!" I flew out of my chair, but my father took my arm. "Let me go."

"The man should live long enough for you to take up to seventy-two hours." Before either of us could respond, he vanished.

"What the fuck was that?" I ripped my arm from his grasp. "We aren't giving him Ivy!" Apollo was a fucking lunatic, that much was for sure. "Where the hell did he go?"

"Everything has to be a show with him." He rubbed the back of his neck and looked at the shattered window. "You're right. We aren't giving him Ivy."

∼

AFTER GETTING CLEANED UP, I followed my dad down the long hall I was becoming way too familiar with. I wanted to leave to go back home, but he said there was someone we needed to meet with first.

"We'll be able to talk more openly once we're in the house. The staff knows about everything." He hadn't been able to look me in the eye since we left the interrogation room.

We had just begun mending our relationship, but this was putting another divide between us. I couldn't trust him, and it was slowly eating away at me. A child should be able to trust their parents.

"I want answers to all my questions." I probed at my nose with my finger as we walked, wondering if it was even healing straight. It had still been swollen when I'd gone to the bathroom to wash the blood from my face.

"I'll do my best." He opened the door into the house and waited for me to pass through in front of him. "Do you want something to eat?"

I gaped at him. "No. I don't want anything to fucking eat. I want to know why you just stood there and let that fucker make a fool of you! I want to know why you care more about this..." I gestured around, referring to the coalition. "... than your own flesh and blood?"

He headed for the kitchen. "What would you have liked me to do, Silas?"

"Tell him no. And before you tell me he'd kill us... don't you think he would have already?" I rushed to keep up with him.

"He had a twinkle in his eye. He's enjoying playing cat and mouse." The kitchen was empty when we entered and he went to the refrigerator, pulling out a whole chicken. "Do you still like rotisserie chicken?"

"Why does none of this bother you? Do you not

have a soul anymore?" My mouth watered as he lifted the cover and the aroma of spices and meat hit my nose. Damn it. He'd picked the chicken on purpose. He knew it was my weakness.

He put the glass container on the counter next to me. "Look. I know it's difficult to understand why I'm not worried right now, but this isn't my first time dealing with Apollo. He moonlights as an agent, but only a few of us know who he actually is."

"And that woman?" Yeah. I wasn't letting that one go.

"He doesn't know she's here. They have a strained father daughter relationship." He ripped off a leg and handed it to me. "She's only here because her rank replaces Johnny."

My eyes widened. "He wants to kill Artemis's daughter, but has one of his own?"

"My brother always was thick-skulled." The soft voice came from behind us, and I turned so fast I almost smacked my dad with the chicken leg. It would have been well deserved.

Artemis was not what I was expecting. I'd half expected her to be wearing a white flowing gown with one of those golden leaf crowns on her head. Instead, she wore jeans and a t-shirt that said *I Like Big Bucks and I Cannot Lie*. Her face was devoid of make-up, and her long brown hair was braided down her back. The resemblance between her and Ivy was definitely there, especially in the face shape and eyes. She didn't look old enough to have a grown daughter.

"Artemis." My father bowed as she approached. "I've

waited a long time to meet you. I wish it was under better circumstances."

Her eyes narrowed, and she moved with a swiftness only someone with a lot of skill could. I jumped in front of my father, her hand wrapping around my throat and lifting me off the ground like I weighed nothing.

The sting from her nails digging into my flesh brought tears to my eyes. She quickly released me, and I coughed. I was really getting the shit beat out of me today.

"You'd protect a murderer?" Her eyes glowed silver, and I gulped the urge to whimper. She studied my face like someone might survey a sculpture. "You're one of my fairest companion's offspring."

She backed up several steps, her eyes returning to their previous gray tone. My dad came forward to stand next to me. The man had balls of steel. I was shitting bricks, and he was dealing with these gods and goddesses like they were nothing to worry about.

"We fell in love." He put his hand on my shoulder. "Your brother tried to take my son, and instead, we made a deal. He wanted me to kill your daughter, Ivy, too."

"Griselda has informed me what my brother has done." Artemis put her hand on her hip. If the resemblance didn't prove she was Ivy's mother, the way she was standing certainly did. "Did Baron suffer?"

My dad shook his head, and she nodded. I scratched at my scruff in confusion. That was it? She wasn't going to beat my dad to a pulp or smite him?

She must have sensed my confusion because her face softened. "Child, my entire existence has been nothing but death. I'll deal with my brother in due time, but I can't fault a father for protecting his son. I protected my daughter by letting her go. I would like to meet her."

"I'm not trusting any of you psychopaths around my woman." I bent down and picked up the chicken leg I'd dropped when she'd grabbed me by the throat. "You're all lunatics."

Artemis threw her head back and laughed, the sound making me want to join in. Instead, I shook the chicken leg at her and tried to find the right words to say.

"Thank you. I haven't had peacock in almost thirty years." She took the leg from me and bit into it, not a care in the world that it had just been on the floor. "Mmm."

"Wait. Peacock? You were trying to feed me a majestic bird?" I wheeled around, my hands itching to lay into my father.

"It's the only animal that's allowed to be cooked around here in Artemis's presence." Griselda walked into the kitchen and started fussing over Artemis standing and eating without a proper meal.

"But... a peacock?" I scrunched my nose in disgust.

"It's no different than eating a cow, chicken, or a pig." My father shrugged.

"I don't like peacocks. They remind me of my stepmother." Artemis slammed the half-eaten leg down on the counter, making us all jump. She hit it so hard the bone cracked in half. "I will destroy her for hurting my wolves."

Griselda quickly started cleaning up the mess on the counter. "Please calm down, Artemis. You know it's not good for you to get so angry."

"What do you mean, hurting your wolves? Do you mean us shifters?" I backed up a few steps because her eyes were doing the angry glow again.

"She's behind the Order of the Queen." Her fists clenched at her sides. "And she will pay."

CHAPTER FOUR

Ivy

*D*eath.

It's not something I usually thought much about. Even when things got dicey, I never felt like any of us would die. Even when Silas's throat was torn to shreds and when Cole had a hole through his belly.

But lying next to Cole, hearing him struggling to breathe, I was thinking about it a lot. He might die, and it was all my fault.

The arrow had been aimed at me.

I snuggled closer to him, hoping feeling me near would help him hold on. I couldn't lose him, not now. Not when we were all starting to come together like we were meant to be.

"Ivy?" Silas's voice was music to my ears... well, thoughts. *"I'm home."*

A sense of relief washed over me, and I sat up. "Silas is back!" I wasn't sure if Cole could hear me, but I'd been talking to him off and on for the past hour. Mostly when no one else was in the room.

The bedroom door opened and Sara walked in, shutting the door gently behind her. "Why don't you go downstairs? I'll sit with Cole until you come back up."

"Silas is back?"

"Uh... yes. With Trevor and um..." She bit her lip as she walked to one of the chairs we'd placed on the side of the bed. "Your mother."

"My... what?" My heart stopped, and my mouth felt like I'd been chewing on cotton. "My mother?"

Sara sat down, stretching her leg out in front of her. "They didn't want to bust in here and disturb Cole. Fair warning... she sends off weird vibes."

I carefully scooted to the end of the bed, trying not to jostle Cole too much. "Weird vibes?" I couldn't even think, let alone speak.

"Like, you know, she's powerful, you can sense it by just being near her. But then she's wearing jeans and a shirt about deer." She laughed softly and reached forward to take Cole's pulse. "Go, I'll call you if there's any change."

I left the room with my heart in my throat and my palms sweating. This moment had seemed like it would never come, and now that it had arrived, I didn't know how to feel. There was an odd mix of fear, excitement, and guilt tumbling inside me.

Would this woman even want to build a relationship with me? Was that what I wanted from someone who abandoned me? Was I disrespecting my adoptive parents' memory?

Stop it. They'd want you to build a new family.

Taking a deep breath, I wiped my palms on my pants and walked down the stairs, my shoulders back and my head held high. She was a fucking goddess. I needed to show her I was just as strong as she was.

Only I wasn't.

The second I could see into the living room, my feet refused to move any farther, and I stood gaping at the back of the woman standing at the window looking out at the forest. Her body was shaped like mine and she even stood like I did. My red hair certainly didn't come from her, but I hadn't expected her to have it, anyway.

"Artemis?" My voice was calm, but I couldn't hide the uncertainty there.

She turned around in a blink and looked up at me. Her face shape was similar to mine and her eyes were like staring in a mirror. Jesus, she was beautiful. The most beautiful woman I'd ever seen.

Muttering something in a foreign language that sounded a lot like the language I'd spoken in when I'd become alpha, she walked toward me. My eyes didn't leave hers despite Silas, Trevor, Eli, and Xander being in the room. I'd hardly even noticed them.

"My precious daughter. Come." She held her hand out to me from the landing. When I eyed it warily, she laughed. "I don't bite."

What was the procedure for meeting your biological family? Was I supposed to hug her? I gulped back my emotion and walked down the remaining stairs, taking her outstretched hand.

Her touch immediately calmed my nerves and sent a warmth through me. It felt like I was back at the coalition's headquarters, but stronger. "You're my mother."

"Indeed." She led me to where she had been standing at the window. "These lands have always been special to me. It's one of the first places I let my animals roam freely. Can you feel the energy?"

I wasn't sure what she meant by that. "I'm not sure what it's supposed to feel like. I've always loved nature, though." I bit my tongue to stop myself from saying that I also loved the deer.

"Over time, my animals fed off the energy all around the globe where I'd released them. Some even began shifting into a more agreeable form for survival." She made a humming sound in her throat.

Not more than a minute later, a few deer wandered out of the trees, their eyes on us. I could faintly see my reflection in the window with my jaw hanging open. A flash of me ripping out a deer's throat and feasting on it brought me back down to Earth, and I let go of her hand.

"People keep trying to kill me." I turned to face her. "What kind of shit are you in for having a baby?"

She stayed staring out the window, but her jaw ticked. "Some like to say that I wanted eternal virginity... but that wasn't my choice." She put her hand against the window, a look of longing in her eyes.

"How does a child turn down all the mountains when all her favorite things live nearby?"

"You abandoned me because you didn't want to lose your mountains?" I scoffed and backed up a step. "Unbelievable."

"I left you with your father because if my father knew, he'd have destroyed you and everything else I loved." Her voice had turned angry, and she turned to face me, her eyes molten silver. "My brother will pay for what he's done."

The floor shook a little, and my immediate reaction was to duck under the coffee table or run to a doorway. It stopped as she took a few deep breaths.

Silas cleared his throat. "I hate to interrupt this reunion, but what about Cole?"

It was as if a switch had been flipped in Artemis, and her face lit up. "Ah, yes! I must heal your betrothed." She patted my arm in reassurance and headed for the stairs.

My eyes widened, and I raced after her, everyone else following.

"I tried to heal him and nothing happened." I caught up to her, our strides matching as she turned toward the bedroom. She just knew right where to go.

"My brother shot him with his arrow. Normal healing won't suffice. You have to pull from your connections." The bedroom door opened on its own and I came to a screeching halt. She turned her head and smiled. "Sorry. I forget normal people aren't used to magic."

"Well, I mean... no." Holy fuck. Was I able to open

doors without touching them too? Excitement bubbled up inside me. "Show me."

"I intend to, dear daughter." With a turn that was more suited to wearing a flowing gown, she moved to the side of the bed. "Come."

I looked to my mates for reassurance, and all they did was heighten my wariness. "What are we doing exactly?"

Sara had already stood and was peeling back the bandages. "We tried several times to repair the damage, but it wouldn't work."

"Thank you, dear." Her eyes traveled down to Sara's prosthetic leg. "Much of your anguish will be healed if you let your wolf run free. She will adapt if you give her time."

Sara gaped at her because her leg wasn't even showing. "Uh, thanks?"

She patted Sara's head and turned to Cole. "Dear daughter, come and let me show you."

Moving next to her, I took a deep breath as she held my hand and plunged it into Cole's open chest. She guided my hand over his lung and warmth spread down my arm to the damaged organ.

"Focus on the connection you have with your other three mates and let their energy flow to you." I didn't know what the hell she was talking about, so I shut my eyes. "Conjure their images in your mind and you will find them."

Tendrils of golden light appeared in my vision, and I reached for them, letting them wrap around me. A surge of undeniable power and strength traveled from the center of my body, down my arm, and to my hand.

"Good. Now focus on mending him." Her hand was still over mine. "That's it. Now, this last part is tricky because we don't want his beautiful body to scar. You must go slowly."

A small growl escaped at her commentary on Cole's body, and she laughed. I opened my eyes as she guided my hand and quickly shut them because the image was too gruesome.

Minutes passed and then her hand left mine. I looked to find a completely closed chest. Cole's skin was no longer pale and his cheeks were rosy like he'd gotten too much sun.

"Perfect!" She clapped her hands in glee and threw her arms around me. I went stiff and patted her arm. "You're a natural."

Eli, Silas, and Xander stood at the end of the bed, shock and wonder written across their faces. They didn't look like anything had happened to them, despite me drawing from their energy or whatever the hell I'd done.

"When will he wake up?"

"Soon." Artemis walked to the window, pulling open the curtains and blinds to let light in. "My friends are here! I will be outside when you're ready to learn more."

And then she disappeared.

Artemis's friends she'd referred to were about one hundred deer that had descended on our yard. When I'd looked out the window and spotted her lying in the center of the yard with them surrounding her, I nearly shifted and jumped through the window.

I guessed my wolf still liked deer.

"Come sit." Eli was sitting next to the bed with Xander. It had been almost an hour and Cole still hadn't woken. "Both of you."

Silas was sitting against the closed bedroom door. "I am sitting."

"Sit closer." Xander grabbed my hand and pulled me onto his lap. "Or lie next to him."

Silas grumbled and then stood, coming to the bed and crawling across to lie next to Cole. "I don't want to hurt him."

"You aren't going to hurt him." I took Cole's hand. "He looks better."

Silas propped himself up on his elbow and looked down at Cole's face. "He's still pretty ugly."

Cole grumbled, his eyes slowly opening and then narrowing at Silas. "Look who's talking." He groaned and his hands lifted to his chest. "What happened?"

Before any of us could speak, Silas threw himself across Cole, a strangled sob leaving him as he buried his face in Cole's shoulder.

Cole put his hand on the back of Silas's head, a look of confusion on his face. "I'm okay, man."

My own tears made an appearance, and Cole's nostrils flared as he looked at me. He brought my hand to his lips, kissing it gently. I scooted off Xander's lap and squeezed into the small space on the end of the bed.

"How are you feeling?" Eli sounded worried still, even though it was clear Cole was completely fine. "Any pain?"

"I'm a little dizzy. It's like I'm going in circles... but not horizontal spinning circles. Vertical ones." Cole's hand stroked my hair. "I don't remember what happened."

"Apollo tried to kill Ivy, and you saved her." Xander stood. "Ivy couldn't heal you until her mom came to help."

"Your... wait. Artemis?" Cole lifted my chin so he could see my face. "Are you okay?"

Was I? I nodded because I didn't want them to know how worried I was. Apollo wasn't going to stop coming after me. Who else was going to be hurt protecting me?

"Our parents are on their way here. I sent Ryan to go get them." Eli leaned forward. "They should be here soon."

Cole groaned. "Man, you know how my mom is."

Silas laughed between his tears. "She's going to make her Coley-poo some soup and kiss his boo-boos all better."

"Pretty much." Cole sat up, lifting us with him. "I feel stronger than usual. What did you guys do to me?"

"I used my mate bond to heal you. I don't exactly know if that gave you some of everyone's strength or what." I caught myself just before I was about to fall off the bed and straightened my shirt. "Let's not think too much about it. Or the fact that I had my hand on your lung."

"Why don't you get cleaned up and I'll go make some food. I'm sure our parents will be hungry when they get here. Do you think Artemis eats meat?" Eli was talking a mile a minute. "I bet she doesn't. I'd go ask, but frankly, she scares me."

"I think she's charming." Xander fought a smile and leaned down, kissing me gently before turning to Eli. "Let's go make sure all of our dildos are put away."

"Well, now I'm not okay." Cole extracted himself from me and Silas and scooted out from in between us. "I could really use a bath."

The door clicked shut after Eli and Xander. I scooted over to Silas, wrapping my arms around him. "I'm glad you're okay." Cole gave me a questioning look. "Apollo took him."

"The guy is fucking bonkers. It was like some joke to him." Silas ran a hand over his face. "There's a prison or something. That's where I woke up."

"For wolves?" My eyes widened, and I looked between Cole and Silas. "Could that be where so many missing wolves end up?"

Silas shrugged. "Possibly. It's something to look into. There was also a woman there... your fox shifter, coalition agent cousin."

Cole whistled. "Damn."

"Who... Apollo's daughter?" My face twisted in disgust. "He's trying to kill his sister's daughter, yet he has one of his own?"

"Apollo isn't a god of chastity." Cole grabbed my hand and pulled me up. "Come take a bath with me."

My arms went around his neck as he pulled me flush against his body. "That seems a little risky with your parents about to show up."

He scoffed. "Silas will lock the door on his way out. I'm a thirty-four-year-old man. I can enjoy a bath with my girlfriend."

Silas headed for the door. "I should probably go find where my father ran off to."

"Or..." Cole's hand tightened on my hip. "You can take a bath with us."

Silas paused with his hand on the door handle. "Is the bath big enough for all three of us?"

"If you want it to be." Cole's thumb rubbed against my skin, and I shivered at the unspoken words of it. "Lock the door, Si."

We headed into the bathroom, the click of the bedroom door louder than it should have been. Sweet baby fawn.

CHAPTER FIVE

Cole

One minute, I remembered staring up at the sky. The next, I was staring up at a pair of worried eyes. I'd almost died yet again. It was becoming a bimonthly ordeal, and I wondered who exactly I'd pissed off to keep coming within an inch of my life.

Flicking on the bathroom light, I turned and grabbed Ivy around the waist and pulled her to me. Her hands rested on my chest, tears in her eyes.

"Cole..." A tear dropped down her cheek, and I leaned forward and kissed it. "You saved me. If you hadn't..."

"Shh. That's what I'm here for." I kissed her other cheek. "I'll start wearing a bulletproof vest when I'm with you."

She laughed through her tears and put her cheek against my chest. "That's not funny."

"It was pretty funny." Silas stood in the doorway, his arms braced on either side of it. "We'd all die for you, you know that, right?"

"I don't want that," she whispered. I tilted her chin up and looked into her pain-filled eyes. "I don't want to see any of you hurt or..."

Silas walked across the room and stood behind her, his hands resting on her hips. "You'd do the same for us, bunny."

We stood for a few minutes together. Hugging was great and all, but I needed more. Some instinctual part of me needed to be with her in any way I could.

Letting her go, I turned on the shower and adjusted the temperature. "I think a shower might be better."

"But you love baths." Silas hopped up on the counter and pulled Ivy between his legs, her back to his front. "Don't let me third-wheeling put a damper on your tub time fun."

I turned and looked at both of them watching me. I didn't exactly know what the fuck I was doing encouraging Silas to join us, but the thought of the three of us together made my cock jump in my boxers.

Their eyes traveled downward, locking on my erection that ached to be free. Without another thought, I pushed them down, my cock springing up to hit my lower belly.

Silas rubbed a hand down his face. "Christ."

"Hm?" I stroked myself a few times, my eyes darting

between the two of them. "I'm going to need some help in the shower."

Ivy practically leapt forward, hastily removing her clothes. She stepped into the shower after me, a mischievous glint in her eyes.

I turned back to Silas, who hadn't gotten off the counter. "I'll need more help than just one set of hands."

I grinned as I turned back to Ivy standing under the stream of water. She was gloriously naked and wet. My muscles relaxed as I dipped under the water with her.

"What are you up to, Cole?" She grabbed a rag and squirted body wash onto it.

"Exploring the possibilities." I kissed her gently and shut my eyes as she began cleaning my chest in small methodical circles. "Life is too short to just think about what could happen."

"You're right." Silas's voice was right next to me, and it made me hold my breath in anticipation. "Keep your eyes shut."

I heard the sound of a bottle opening and then his hands were on my head, massaging my scalp. I'd never really given much thought to what being intimate with another man would be like, but I wasn't opposed.

Ivy moved farther and farther down my body with the rag, taking her sweet time to clean every crevice of my abdomen. When she reached my dick, she avoided it, cleaning my legs instead.

Silas guided my head back and rinsed my hair, his fingers brushing over my forehead to block the shampoo from running into my eyes. His fingers trailed down my face and ghosted over my lips, and I moaned.

What was happening to me?

"This is what you want?" His voice was as soft as his light touches across my collarbone. Completely unexpected from him.

"Is it what you want?" I stopped his hand from moving. "I'm not asking for marriage, sweetheart."

"Oh, shut the fuck up." His other hand pinched my nipple, and I gasped, my cock jerking and my pulse racing. "Hm, daddy liked that."

"You fucker. Don't call me that." I nearly choked on the words because at that exact moment, a warm mouth surrounded my throbbing dick. "Oh, fuck."

I let go of Silas's hand and found Ivy's head, grabbing the back of it and guiding her as she swallowed me whole.

My body was sent backward until I was against the cool tiles. Silas was watching Ivy as she sucked and licked me like it was the last blow job she'd ever give.

"Come here, Silas." My voice was low and shaking. Fuck. I was going to do this, wasn't I? "Let me feel what drives our woman crazy."

Taking a deep breath, he stepped forward, angling himself at my side. "I don't know about this."

I saw the heat in his eyes, so I went for it. I wrapped my hands around his dick as if it were my own. Ivy was watching us intently, and she hummed around my dick in satisfaction.

Silas and I stared at each other for a moment before

I gave his cock a long, firm stroke with my fist. His eyes shut and his breath came out shaky.

"Look at me while I get you off." I put my head back against the wall as Ivy's hand massaged my balls. I wasn't going to last long.

Silas opened his eyes and braced an arm next to my head as I jerked him slowly. His pupils were nearly blown, and his body trembled. "Don't stroke me like I'm a delicate flower."

"Don't tell me how to jack you off." I rubbed my thumb over his head and he turned his mouth against his arm. "Does it feel good?"

He shook his head. It very damn well did, judging from his hard nipples and the pre-cum dripping from his slit.

My hand stroked harder, matching the pace of Ivy's mouth. Every movement she made brought me closer and closer to the edge.

"Yes, baby. Just like that." I resisted the urge to thrust my hips and bury myself farther down her throat. "Fuck."

Silas leaned forward and took my nipple between his teeth, and my entire body lit up like a firecracker had gone off at the base of my spine. I exploded in Ivy's mouth, shooting down her throat.

Warmth hit my leg and Silas gasped around my nipple before letting go and keeping his head against my pec. We stood there panting, my hand still stroking his dick until every drop was spilled.

Ivy released me with a pop and stood, looking between the two of us. "That was hot." She stepped under the water, her hands playing with her nipples. "Now with all four of you crossing swords, my jaw can finally get a little vacation."

My shoulders shook as I laughed, Silas joining me and pulling away from where he'd rested his head against my chest. His cheeks were red, and he met my eyes briefly before looking away.

Was he going to be weird now?

Ivy reached for the shower wand and adjusted the temperature and stream of water. "My turn."

"Ugh, bunny." Silas reached for her and she batted him away. "You have two strapping young men right here with dicks and tongues."

"Mm. Yes." She lowered it down her body. "Hold my leg up for me."

My dick was already getting hard again as she leaned against the wall and lifted her leg. Silas complied with a grumble and held her leg under the knee.

With one hand, she pulled her pussy lips apart, and with the other, she held the water a few inches from her clit. Her mouth opened, her head falling back against the wall. I'd never watched her get herself off before, and as much as I wanted to be the one doing it, there was something intimate and sexy about watching her pleasure herself.

Her body was already trembling, and her eyes met mine. "Cole." She cried out as her orgasm hit her, her leg nearly giving out as she practically doubled over.

I grabbed her around the waist, holding her up and taking her lips to claim as my own. Her shudders continued as our tongues tangled in a feverish kiss that left me harder than a rock.

The shower wand hit the wall with a clunk, and then Silas wrapped his hand around my shaft. "I think she's ready for your cock." He guided me toward Ivy's entrance, her leg still held up and open for me.

I sank inside her, her wet heat clenching around me as I buried myself to the hilt. "Fuck. It's like coming home." I kissed down to her neck, nipping and sucking as I thrust in and out of her.

Silas kissed the opposite side of her neck, his hand covering hers as he guided it to his dick. "You're lucky I'm about ready to explode again, or I'd be buried inside you right alongside him."

His words brought memories of us both sliding into her tight cunt. That needed to happen again. Soon. I was so fucking turned on by the two of them that my head was spinning with my building orgasm.

"Come with me," I growled into her neck, grinding my pelvis against hers to hit all the right spots.

"Cole! Yes!" Her mouth opened in a silent scream as she squeezed around me.

"That's it, bunny. Milk his cock." Silas bit out each word, his hand working with Ivy's in overdrive as they worked in tandem to get him off. His cum shot from him, hitting our sides.

"Fuuuuuck me." I spilled inside her, my vision practically exploding with stars as pleasure spread all over my body.

It was just what I needed to remember I was alive.

I DIDN'T WANT to leave the bedroom but knew my parents would arrive soon. The last thing I needed was for them to hear me having a good time upstairs. Not that you could hear much downstairs, but at the rate we were going, there'd be a lot more noise.

I pulled on a fresh pair of jeans and looked up at Ivy pulling on her own. Her hair was still wet from the shower, dampening the back of her t-shirt.

She looked over at me and smiled. "What?"

"Just thinking about how perfect you are." I pulled on a gray shirt and ran my fingers through my hair. "Now before you meet my folks…"

"His mom is a mother hen. I haven't seen her in a long ass time, but my guess is nobody's good enough for her baby boy. Not even the alpha demi-goddess that can hit a bullseye and heal with the touch of a hand." Silas finished tying his shoes at the end of the bed and jumped up.

"She's not that bad." She *was* a little too involved. I loved her to death, though. "Anytime I brought a girl home growing up, she'd ask them so many questions that I swear that's why we never had more than a couple of dates."

"I don't think your mom had anything to do with that." Silas smirked and pulled his shirt on. "But maybe you were just holding out for Ivy. I know I was."

"Honestly, I've been a serial dater too." She wrapped her arms around my waist and put her head against my chest, her wet hair making a spot on my shirt. "But this is right. We're right."

I was about to tell her I agreed, but then yelling and a loud crash came from downstairs.

Silas cringed and looked at the door. "Oh, yeah. My dad's here too."

"You guys better get down here." Eli sounded nervous, and I rushed to the door, throwing it open.

"Stop it, Walter!" My mom's voice was raised as the sound of glass shattering came from the living room. "Trevor! No!"

"Shit." I ran down the stairs, Silas close behind, nearly colliding with Xander who was sitting a few steps from the bottom, his arms wrapped around his legs. I couldn't tell if he was enjoying the show or internally freaking out.

"Hey! Stop!" I went right to them on the pile of what used to be the coffee table. How they'd managed to break a solid piece of furniture that was sturdy—I'd fucked Ivy on top of it—was beyond my comprehension.

I grabbed for my dad as he hauled his arm back to punch Trevor in the face again. He was strong as a bull, and his arm slipped through my grip, slamming into Trevor's jaw. A splatter of blood flew from his mouth and nose, getting all over my area rug.

"Enough!" Ivy's growl came from behind me and both men stiffened before my dad snapped around, pinning Ivy with a glare which only made her stand taller. "Stop fighting. You're damaging our house."

My dad's eyes landed on me, a blaze of fury in them,

and I braced myself. I hadn't exactly told them that everyone, including my girlfriend, had moved into my house.

"Who the hell are you?" My dad stood to his full height, a few inches taller than me, and Ivy audibly inhaled. He was a big man and even though he was a retired alpha, he still exuded alpha energy.

"I'm Ivy, the alpha of this pack, and you're in my territory damaging my property and injuring my guests." Her voice was strong, and I bit my lip to stop myself from grinning from ear to ear.

It was exciting to see my girlfriend stop two alpha men from killing each other and then tell off my dad. I'd ignore the fact that I couldn't break the fight up myself.

"Your property?" He looked at me. "You said you had a girlfriend."

"I do." I wrapped my arm around her waist and tugged her closer. "She's my mate."

"Your..." He pinched the bridge of his nose.

"She's my mate too." Silas joined us, holding her waist from the other side. "She has four mates, and we all live here together. Sometimes we all fuck her at the same time too. In fact, Cole and I just-" Ivy put her hand over his mouth.

My mom gasped, bringing a shaking hand to her mouth. I was just now noticing her behind us, standing over by the fireplace next to Eli's dad, Juan. Why the fuck were they standing so close?

"What's going on here?" My eyes traveled down to where Juan was holding my mom's hand. "Mom?"

Eli must have just seen what I did because he made a strangled noise in the back of his throat. "Are you... oh my God." He sat down on the stairs next to Xander. "When you said you met someone..."

"It wasn't a complete lie. I'd just met a different side of her. Well, them. It just kind of happened." Juan laughed like it wasn't a big deal our parents were together. "It certainly surprised me."

"Hello! I heard our parents were-" Sara came to a screeching halt once she could see everyone. "What the hell is this?"

"Love. You can't fight who you may fall in love with." Artemis was right behind Sara and walked up to Trevor and stuck her hand on his face, healing him instantly. "What's for dinner?"

Chaos erupted, and everyone started talking at once. Xander quickly retreated up the stairs, Eli staring after him. My dad was glaring at Trevor again. Ivy was laughing at something with Silas.

The sudden urge to cry came over me, and a laugh bubbled out of me before I plopped down in a chair and put my head in my hands. Everything was a fucking mess, and now on top of it, there were parents involved.

A soft hand stroked the back of my neck. I knew it was my mom without even looking up. Her scent enveloped me, making my little hysterical outburst even worse. I turned into her, wrapping my arms around her waist and putting my head against her soft belly.

"You're okay." She stroked my hair, and the room

fell silent. "Why don't you nitwits go figure out what's for dinner. I'm starving."

Everyone except Ivy followed Eli to the kitchen, where discussion about dinner started in earnest. I swear someone asked if we had any peacocks.

"That includes you, dear." My mom's voice was gentle, but I could hear the anger in her tone. "You've caused enough damage here."

I stiffened and pulled back, looking up at my mom. "Mom, Ivy's-"

"Oh, I know her type. She broke you, son." She wiped my cheek with her thumb.

I flinched and looked at Ivy, who looked ready to cry herself, but she gulped down her emotions. "Ma'am, I love your son."

"He wasn't a blubbering mess when we left, but he meets you, and here he is, crying his eyes out." She glared at Ivy, and my heart deflated.

"Mom." I stood and went to Ivy's side. "I'm just overwhelmed. I was just shot with an arrow."

My chest suddenly felt like it was on fire, and I rubbed it. Damn it. Maybe I was turning into a puddle of goo.

"Let me see." My mom grabbed the hem of my shirt, and I batted her hand away. "How bad is the wound? Eli made it sound like you were about to die."

"Well, I was, but..."

"We healed him." Artemis, who I hadn't met, but who else could she be, came into the room and flopped on the couch. She was eating an entire crown of raw broccoli. "You're welcome."

My mom's hands went to her hips. "Who are you?"

"Who I am is of little importance." She took a large bite of broccoli and chewed it as we all watched in awe. "What's important is I helped heal your son, free of charge might I add, which means you don't get to talk to my daughter that way."

Great. Was a cat fight going to break out now? My mom had some claws, but she couldn't take on a goddess.

"This is my mom... Martha." Ivy wrung her hands in front of her. "Mom, this is..."

"Martha." My mom rolled her eyes and threw her hands in the air. "Just perfect. We have the same name."

I threw my head back and laughed. This was such a train wreck, and I was thinking about going and hiding out with Xander upstairs.

"You could have picked a better name, dear. Martha is old and stuffy." Artemis stood, throwing the stem of the broccoli on the broken coffee table. "I'm Artemis, goddess of all things pure."

"What kind of crazy did you invite into this house, Cole Elliot?" My mom using my middle name made me want to run away and hide somewhere. It didn't matter how old I was, it made me feel like I'd just committed murder.

"The kind that I love." I grabbed Ivy's hand and brought it to my lips. "And soon you will too."

CHAPTER SIX

Ivy

*H*aving all the parents sitting with us around the dining room table for dinner had been more nerve-wracking than expected. One minute things were going fine, and the next Trevor and Walter were in an argument.

Then there were the mothers. It was a battle of who could glare at the other the hardest. Cole's mom really loved Cole, but she hated me from the moment she saw me.

"You all right?" Eli had barely eaten any of his food. It didn't help that when he'd started to eat along with everyone else, Cole's father had stared at him in shock.

"I will be if you eat." I took the last bite of my pasta. "Screw what he thinks. If he's still hungry, he can go eat the broccoli stem Artemis threw out on the coffee table."

Eli laughed under his breath and popped a piece of chicken in his mouth. "I don't know whether to laugh or cry."

"Same." I took a gulp of my wine, and Silas immediately refilled it. It seemed like an excellent occasion to drink too much.

"I'm going to go for a stroll." Artemis stood from the table, her salad, pasta, and bread demolished. Silas had filled all of us in through our connection about her aversion to all meat except peacock.

I was sure that someone was going to jump out with cameras and say I was on a hidden camera prank show. How was this my life?

"I'll go with you." I followed her to the back door, hearing a few chairs move back from the table. "Alone."

I gave them a reassuring look and followed Artemis out onto the deck. It was already dark out, but the deer grazing on the lawn were easily visible from the lights in the house filtering out the windows and the moon shining.

"This was a bad idea." I went to turn, but she grabbed my hand. "My wolf has a taste for deer."

"I know." She pulled me along with her. "The deer told me."

"They told you?" I gaped at her as we went down the deck steps. "But... how?"

We walked across the grass toward the trees, hand in hand. Something about it felt so natural and so right that tears came to my eyes. "Why'd you leave me?"

She didn't speak until we were in the woods. I knew the guys wouldn't be happy we were out of eyesight, but this was my mother, and so far, she'd given no sign of wanting to hurt me.

Once the lights from the house could barely be seen, she plopped down right on the forest floor, yanking me down with her. We sat across from each other, my hands in hers.

"I knew that even if my father accepted what I'd done, raising you in the world I live in wasn't what was best. You needed a pack and someone that could be with you throughout all your years. I did what I thought was right." She made a humming noise and small lights flickered in the forest.

I looked around, amazed. I didn't even know California had lightning bugs, but apparently when Artemis was around, they came out. Or it was magic.

"You didn't even want to see me? To visit? Didn't you care that Baron was killed?" If I'd found out my love was murdered, I would have been back in an instant, seeking answers.

She patted my hand. "I've been asleep for the past twenty-six years. It was easier to keep away. Something pulled me awake, and now I know that something was you."

"But... I needed you then." A tear slid down my cheek.

"You need me now." She squeezed my hands in such a tender way I bit my lip to stop the floodgates from opening. "Griselda said you were raised well, by loving parents. Did she lie?"

"No, but-"

"But nothing, sweet child. Everything in this universe happens for a reason. It was written in the stars that I shouldn't bear a child. The consequence of that was the death of your father. I can't fault Trevor for doing what was best for his own child." A wistful look crossed her face. "Baron was a good man, too. The only one I'd ever wanted to give myself to."

"Now what? We wait around for Apollo to come try to kill me again?" My jaw clenched in anger. "He almost killed my mate."

"Apollo is complicated. He means well, but his first reaction is always to kill now, ask questions later. Many wars have started because of that." She laughed, and I found myself staring at her with an open mouth again. "He's run off to do who knows what. When he returns, I'll take care of him. The more pressing issue is this group of zealots kidnapping wolves in the name of Hera. Hera has not left Mount Olympus for at least a millennium."

"What?" There was so much about what she just shared that I needed to unpack and process. "Hera? Zeus's wife? Mount Olympus?"

"Yes, my evil step grandmother." She looked around as if she thought we were being listened to and then lowered her voice. "She hates all of his children that didn't come from her womb."

I opened my mouth and then snapped it closed. What was I supposed to say to that? To know that Xander's suffering was because of a beef a goddess had with her husband infuriated me.

"Is she behind it?" If we were dealing with a goddess, the top dog of them all, what chance did we have?

"I'm not entirely sure. It wouldn't surprise me if she was pulling strings from afar. Over the years she has had some rabid followers that act in her name, thinking she's going to grace them with her presence and make them immortal." She shrugged. "I've only been awake since this morning, so it's too early to tell what their motivation is."

A quietness circled around us as the lightning bugs flitted around in the trees. It was peaceful sitting on the forest floor with this woman I'd barely met. Power oozed off her, but she didn't strike me as dangerous or having bad intentions.

"How could you have been asleep for so long? It's called stasis?" A fawn and its mother approached, and I stiffened. I had my wolf under control for the most part, but around deer, all bets were off.

Artemis let go of one of my hands and waited for the fawn to come nuzzle her hand. I didn't feel the urge to eat either of the deer, but if I did, what would my mother think?

"I know you're part wolf. Just don't kill my hinds and I won't be angry." She pulled the fawn into her lap like it was a puppy, stroking its head and back. "Sleeping for that long is normal for us. Some of us choose to sleep for longer because it rejuvenates us and keeps us youthful. I will have to show you how to do it after we build you the proper place to rest."

"Um." The mother deer was sniffing my hair, and I batted her away. "I don't want to go into a stasis."

"You wish to grow old and perish?" A line formed between her eyebrows. "You could live forever if you choose."

My eyes widened. "What do you mean?"

"All the halfling sons and daughters can preserve their lives indefinitely with the proper care."

"What about my mates?"

"The dryad can if he goes into his tree form."

I nearly choked on the air I was breathing. "His tree form? Excuse me?"

"He can merge his life with a tree. Did you not know this? His mother was a wood nymph." She lifted the fawn from her lap and stood. "Call him to you, and I'll show you. It's simple really. He just needs to find a tree he connects with and merge his life force with it. Full-blooded dryads can actually grow the tree themselves if they wish."

Blinking up at her, I didn't know what the hell to think. Was it possible I was imagining everything since earlier today as a coping mechanism?

The possibility of outliving my mates by hundreds of thousands of years made my chest hurt. They would age while I took long naps, and for what? Wandering the Earth alone once they were gone?

"Let's just go back to the house. I'm not feeling too well." I stood, ignoring that the mother deer and her fawn followed when I started to walk.

"Tomorrow then." She sounded dejected.

I turned, and she nearly ran right into me. "It's just a

lot to take in. I think I need to sleep on it and talk to my mates. Right now, we really have bigger issues to deal with than my lifespan."

"Ah, yes. Tomorrow we'll train." A grin spread across her face. "Then my brother and any other threat will think twice about messing with the daughter of Artemis."

The daughter of Artemis.

Holy shit.

~

Sleeping with four men sounded good in theory, but when it came to reality, it wasn't all it was glammed up to be in the romance novels. Sure, it was nice to always have someone there to keep me company, but sometimes I questioned the decision to buy a gigantic family-sized bed.

Instead of one potential snorer, there were four. Sometimes all four would drink and the room would sound like a pig farm. And the smells... the smells were the worst.

Which was exactly why I was moving to my own bedroom in the middle of the night. I needed sleep, and being sandwiched between four snoring men wasn't helping.

Voices from downstairs made me pause as I walked across the hall toward my bedroom. It was nearly two in the morning and everyone had left hours ago. Cole's parents and Eli's dad left for the house down the road, Trevor went back to the coalition's headquarters, and Artemis was set up in the guest room downstairs.

I crept down the stairs, Artemis's voice becoming more recognizable. But the other voice, I didn't know. Once they came into view, I opened my mouth to scream, but with a swipe of his hand, Apollo silenced me. It was as if I had lost my voice, and no matter how hard I tried, all that came out was air.

I tried to move, finding that I was stuck in place, like my feet were encased in cement. I couldn't even connect to my mates.

"Apollo." Artemis moved between us and faced away from me. "Be nice."

He had just magically muzzled and restrained me and all she had to say was 'be nice'?

"I'm not going to hurt her, Art. She was about to scream. I hate screamers. Well, unless it's in the bedroom." He smirked, and if I could have cringed, I would have. He looked my age, but hearing him talk about sex was like hearing your parents talk about it.

If my mates couldn't hear my scream, then they would be able to hear my racing heart. Except they were snoring so loudly they probably couldn't hear a thing.

"She won't scream." Artemis looked over her shoulder. "Will you?" I couldn't exactly answer her and she laughed. "Oh, well. Don't scream, please."

This was exactly why I needed sleep. Shit was too weird for it to be real. I'd seen a lot in the past few months, but this was a whole other level.

My body unfroze, and I clamped my mouth shut. I

tried to reach out to the guys but hit a wall. "What do you want?"

"I came to kill you, but my dear sister spoiled all the fun." Apollo walked to the mantle above the fireplace and picked up a picture of Eli and Silas spooning in bed. "You allow your males to indulge in each other?"

"That's none of your business." I didn't move from my spot on the stairs, even though I really wanted to snatch the photo from him. It had appeared on the mantle one day, and Eli and Silas had chased Cole around the house for ten minutes for taking it.

"Four males." He put the photo back and went to the window. The forest was dark and the lamp in the living room made it hard to see anything outside. "You can spare me one then."

These gods were nuts. "I think you need to leave."

"She's not giving you one of her males. They're her mates and she needs them. Don't you have anything better to do, like run your precious coalition?" Artemis was starting to sound angry, and I wondered if another fight was about to break out in the living room. This time more than just a coffee table would be damaged.

Screaming was an option, but then they'd come downstairs and would take Silas. I could totally handle two crazy gods.

"You need to leave my daughter alone. I'll deal with father when and if he has an issue with my promiscuity." Artemis went to her brother and put her hand on his crossed arms. "You worry about me too much."

"He could take everything from you." He looked at

me still standing on the stairs, ready to run if I needed to. "Is she worth it?"

"She's worth everything." She patted his cheek and stepped back. "I challenge you to a duel tomorrow to settle this once and for all. If I win, you leave my daughter, her males, and her pack alone. If you win, you can take the dreamy blonde one."

"What? No!" My wolf nearly burst free, ready to rip both of them to shreds. "He's not taking Silas!"

Before I could stop her, she stretched out her hand and took Apollo's. As soon as their palms connected, light filled the room, and I shielded my eyes.

What had she just done?

~

I STARED AT THE CEILING, my eyes heavy with sleep, but unable to find that peaceful place where everything went away. It was becoming harder and harder to stay optimistic.

Would it be cowardly of me to run? My mates could come with me, and we could start over somewhere new and forget any of this even existed.

Except I couldn't. The OQ potentially had hundreds of wolves and were probably plotting to make their move soon. I couldn't leave my pack and the other packs behind because my biological family had issues.

I rolled over and looked out the window. Seeing the outdoors usually helped me fall asleep, but I wanted to be lying out in the yard, gazing up at the full moon.

Speaking of which, I needed to ask my mother

about pregnancy. I'd gotten a birth control implant, but that still didn't ease my worries that it would work on a demi-goddess wolf shifter.

"Ivy, where are you?" Even through our connection, Eli sounded like he'd just woken up.

"In my bedroom." I focused on him and sensed him move closer. I'd been working on using the unique bond we had, but it also required me to think about it. It didn't come naturally when I was focused on so many other things.

The door opened, and his scent wrapped around me like a warm blanket. The bed dipped as he laid down and wrapped his arms around me.

"What's wrong?" His hand settled on my hip and his cheek rubbed against mine. "My wolf missed you."

"Couldn't sleep." I wondered if I should even tell him about what had transpired downstairs. We'd had a big discussion about not keeping secrets from each other. "Artemis and Apollo will be dueling this morning."

"What?" His cheek stopped nuzzling me and his hand tightened on my hip. "When did this happen?"

"A few hours ago. If Artemis wins, then he has to leave us alone. If Apollo wins... he gets Silas." I rolled over and took in his pained expression. "I won't let that happen."

"What are we going to do?" He brought his hand to my cheek, and I nuzzled against it. "Can we kill him?"

Could we? I had two of his arrows; the one he shot Cole with and the one he shot at me when he was running. It was a promising idea, but if it failed, it would only piss the god off more.

I shook my head. "We aren't doing anything. I'll think of something. I want you four to stay out of this mess."

"We're in it together. We've told you that we face everything together." He ran his fingers across my lips and then down to my collarbone. His touches were making me sleepy. "Promise me."

"I promise to protect you." My eyes shut as his fingers danced across my cleavage and then down my arm to thread our fingers together. "Promise me if I ever get as crazy as them, you'll lock me up."

He kissed my forehead with a chuckle. "I promise to join you."

I drifted off to sleep, hoping that in a few hours we'd be able to rest easier again.

CHAPTER SEVEN

Eli

My heart ached as I watched Ivy drift off to sleep in my arms. Watching someone feel like they needed to carry the weight of the world on their shoulders was tough. There were four of us to help her bear the pressure on her, but she chose to shoulder it alone.

The sun rose faster than I would have liked, and I slipped out of bed, leaving her to sleep for a few more hours. We all could have used a few extra hours of sleep, but the night before when Ivy was outside with Artemis, Trevor had insisted we meet with him privately at sunrise.

The others were already waiting downstairs in various states of awake. I kissed Xander on the temple as he took a drink of his coffee and went to the cupboard to get my mug.

"She all right?" Silas was sitting on the counter, a half-eaten banana in his hand.

"Apollo was here."

They growled, and I smiled. If he wasn't a god that could probably send our heads flying with a punch, we'd have killed him already. "There's going to be a duel today between him and Artemis. If Apollo wins, then Artemis said he can take Silas."

I poured coffee in my travel mug as Silas choked on the bite of banana he'd just swallowed. Cole beat him on the back as he coughed and turned red.

"He isn't taking Silas," Xander growled. "He's not hurting Ivy either. How do we kill a god?"

"You don't," Trevor said as he walked across the living room to the kitchen. "You can incapacitate him for a while, but that will only piss him off. The last thing we want is a pissed off god."

"How the hell did you get in here?" Cole snatched the box of donuts he was carrying. "There better be an apple fritter."

"Of course." Trevor sat on the barstool next to Xander, putting a hand on his shoulder. My wolf bristled. "How are you doing today?"

Xander shrugged off his hand and stood. "I'm peachy."

An awkward silence filled the kitchen as we all grabbed a donut and ate them. Trevor was trying, but it was hard to forget he'd gone AWOL for years with no word to his son. Not to mention he was a murderer.

He had been protecting Silas the only way he knew how, but it didn't change the fact that there was one less wolf in the world because of it. His only saving grace was he'd protected Ivy.

"Is there somewhere more private we can discuss what I wanted to meet with you four about?" He looked over at the stairs.

That didn't sound ominous at all.

"We can go to the conference room." Cole shoved the last bit of his apple fritter in his mouth and led us to the empty den.

Whatever he was going to tell us had my wolf on edge. We weren't supposed to be keeping secrets, and meeting with him without Ivy was exactly that. How could we expect her not to act on her own when we were doing it?

With a heavy sigh, I sat in a chair and sipped my coffee. As soon as we were done, I planned on telling Ivy everything. It was the only way our relationship was going to continue to grow.

"Thank you for being discreet about this," Trevor started as soon as Cole had shut the door. "I know it can be difficult to keep things from the ones you love." He stared at Silas.

"Get on with it." Silas scratched at something crusted on the table. "We don't have all day. Artemis and Apollo are fighting for my freedom."

Trevor's frown deepened. "He's not going to take you, son. I promise you that."

"Your promises mean nothing." Silas leaned back in his chair, crossing his arms.

Cole cleared his throat. "What did you want to talk to us about?"

"The OQ." He leaned forward with his hands on the table, looking at each one of us. "We located their main compound."

"That's great. When do we go kick their asses?" Silas stood, but then plopped back down when Trevor held up his hand to stop him. "We are going to kick their asses, right?"

"It's not as simple as that. This place is in the middle of a major metropolitan area. It would put us at risk of being exposed and put humans in harm's way if the wolves they have escape." He pulled his phone out and put it in the center of the table, pulling up a video and pressing the play button.

A video began to play from inside a large warehouse. There were no windows, but someone had gotten in to get video footage. The image was a little dark because the lights were low, but rows upon rows of cages were filled with wolves.

"How did you get this?" Cole pulled the phone closer, and we all stood behind him to see. "Is there sound?"

"That is the sound. It's quiet. Just wait."

There was a buzzer like a warning for a gate opening, and the cages all opened at the same time. The wolves exited in unison, turned, and all walked in an orderly fashion. My throat felt like it was closing as I watched the wolves march toward an open area. The only sounds were the clicking of nails on the cement floor.

They filed into the area, sitting in nice straight rows with their attention toward a raised platform. It reminded me of soldiers ready to receive their orders.

Whoever or whatever was controlling the video looked around the room. Two men appeared on a platform in front of the gathered wolves. One had his hands behind his back and the other had a shock stick in his hand.

"What the fuck?" Silas whispered and his hand sought out mine. "Is he going to..."

The man with the shock stick hit the other man in the back of the legs, making him fall to his knees. "What do you have to say for yourself?"

"Fuck you!" The man turned his head and tried to spit on him. "I hope you rot in hell."

"Such a shame. You had so much potential." He pushed the man with his boot so he was lying face down on the platform. "Lunch time."

He backed up, and the video cut off. We stared at the screen in disgust and shock. He'd... fed the man to the wolves. Xander had backed against the wall behind us, a stricken look on his face.

I reached for him, and he shook his head. I hated seeing him hurt, but if space was what he needed after seeing that video, then I needed to give him it.

"I didn't think you needed to see the whole thing." Trevor sounded apologetic. "But this is what they do with the wolves they train. We think they have several training facilities to break them in and then they move them to where the video was taken."

"That was what they were trying to do to us. But

they were also trying to find an alpha." Silas ran a hand down his face. "Jesus."

"Are they all shifters?" Cole was still staring at the phone screen that had turned black.

"We believe so." Trevor took his phone back and slid it into his pocket. "We're still gathering intel, but for now they are waiting to use them. They might be gathering more wolves, but we think they've stopped since we infiltrated their last training facility."

"So, what? We're just going to wait? If you know where this place is, we need to move in and save them before they're too far gone." I was squeezing Silas's hand so hard I was surprised he hadn't said something yet.

"There are at least nine hundred wolves. We can't just go in guns blazing. We have an agent trying to learn how they control the cages so we can deactivate them from the outside and ensure none get out to attack. Every time she goes back though, she risks being captured herself." Trevor started pacing the length of the table. "Apollo wants us to wait."

Silas made a noise and let go of my hand, taking the comfort it brought me with it. "And we're going to listen to that lunatic?"

"Apollo is highly skilled. If he wants to wait, then we need to follow his lead." Trevor ran a hand down his face the same way Silas had. They were more similar than Silas probably cared to admit. "He's not a lunatic. He's just lived a very long time and socially is a little inept."

"A little inept? He tried to kill Ivy." Silas rolled his

eyes. "He must give good head to have you singing his praises."

Trevor's nostrils flared, but he didn't respond. That was probably for the best since we didn't need to break up another fight.

"Who's the woman you're sending in? How is she getting so close without them detecting her?" It was a stupid idea to send anyone into a place like that. One misstep and they'd be wolf food or in a cage themselves.

"Agent Carter. She just transferred to our headquarters to assist in the matter." Trevor met Silas's glare. "She's Apollo's daughter."

We were all shocked into silence because the room was so quiet you could hear a pin drop. Cole finally stood. "Is that all you wanted to show us? Why didn't you want Ivy here?"

"Because Ivy doesn't need to see something like that," Xander whispered. "None of us really did."

"Xander's right. She has enough going on. Artemis should also be kept out of this." Trevor walked toward the door. "She's a bit of a loose cannon when it comes to someone abusing her animals."

I snorted. "Seems like a loose cannon all the time. She was eating a whole onion last night like it was an apple."

"We all have our quirks." Trevor opened the door and turned to face us. "For now, it should be safe to go about your normal daily routines. We have agents monitoring all roads in the area. Plus, their main operation is hours from here. I'll show myself out."

We sat in silence for a few minutes after he left. A million thoughts and scenarios went through my head about the OQ. What did they want? Were they going to attack humans? Was Hera behind it all?

"I don't know if I trust his strategy." Silas rested his elbows on the table and put his chin on his folded hands. "Why can't we just hack into whatever system is controlling the cages and disable them?"

"I'd have to get close to the building to see what kinds of signals there are, and that would require knowing where they are. He didn't exactly tell us that." Even if I could disable the cages from the outside, there was no guarantee they didn't have a fail-safe button.

"He said it's in a major metropolitan area, and they had to buy those cages from somewhere. How many places carry something like that?" Cole pulled out his phone. "What would we even search for? Heavy duty animal cages?"

Xander finally returned to us and sat down next to me, scooting close and putting his hand on my thigh. "They are cages for wild animals. Where do zoos get their cages they transport in?"

"They also buy the dog food in bulk. If they were buying pallets for a smaller group, imagine how much they buy for almost a thousand." Silas rubbed the back of his neck. "I remember the brand. We can call some suppliers."

Cole grunted. "I know none of you want to hear this, but we shouldn't do this."

Silas threw his hands in the air in frustration. "We have the manpower. We can call in other packs for backup. Why should we trust the coalition? Look what happened the last time we trusted them."

He was right. If we wanted to save them, we needed to plan on doing it ourselves.

∾

Ivy was up to something, but I couldn't for the life of me figure out what exactly. When we'd gotten back to the house, she was eating a donut and drinking coffee, but instead of asking where we'd been, she'd been quiet.

It was never a good sign when she was quiet.

"I'm going to go work on a project for a bit. I'm not really interested in watching Apollo fight to take me." Silas grabbed another donut. "Xander, are you coming?"

Xander put the lid on his freshly poured coffee. "Yeah. I could use the distraction."

As he walked toward the back door, I snagged him around the waist. "Are you okay?"

"I'm fine. You'll be the first to know if I'm not." He kissed me gently and then followed Silas outside.

"What time is the duel happening?" Cole went to the sink and made a noise of disgust. "Can't anyone rinse their dishes and put them in the dishwasher? Jesus. I swear, I live with children."

Ivy tapped her nails on the counter. She only did that when she was mad about something. "Why were you guys meeting in the conference room with Trevor?"

The dish that Cole was rinsing dropped into the sink. "Fuck."

I was going to wait until after the Artemis and Apollo situation was dealt with, but there was no time like the present. "He wanted to meet with us about some new intel they have. We are safe to go about our daily lives."

"And why wasn't I included in that?" She took another donut and smacked it down on her paper towel. "I felt Xander's distress."

Cole turned, drying his hands on a rag. "They know where the wolves are being kept but are waiting on Apollo to give the go ahead. They don't want Artemis knowing anything about it."

Ivy lowered her voice. "We can't trust them."

"We know that." I put my hand on her shoulder and rubbed her neck with my thumb. "We're going to do some digging to see if we can find out where they are too."

"I think we can trust Artemis. Apollo... not so much." She ripped her donut in half. "He's kind of creepy."

"Now, now. Is that anyway to talk about your favorite uncle?" Apollo appeared out of thin air, making us all jump.

Cole and I moved to put ourselves between him and Ivy, causing him to laugh. "Get out of our house."

"It's funny you think you can protect her from me." He craned his neck to look in the donut box. "Are there any donuts left?"

What the hell was happening? I didn't know

whether we should try to fight the guy or let him be. My wolf had no reaction to him at all, which was annoying because he should have been pawing to get out.

"Good morning, my children." Artemis came into the room with a flourish. "Apollo. You're right on time. Shall we settle things once and for all?"

I didn't exactly know what a duel between two gods entailed, but I wasn't about to sit inside and miss out on watching from the safety of the deck.

CHAPTER EIGHT

Ivy

The day was already warming up as we made our way to the backyard. I didn't know what to expect, but I had my bow and the two special arrows he'd shot hidden in a bush right off the deck.

I couldn't let Apollo win.

"What are your rules, sister?" Apollo looked around the yard.

Artemis rubbed her chin in thought. "Five minutes of hand-to-hand combat, level one abilities only. Once the time is up, we meet back in this exact spot to decide."

"I have one I would like to add." Apollo looked over at me and then at the bush. "Any interference before, during, or after the duel is an automatic disqualification. That includes attempting to harm either of us."

"Sounds as if you're scared of losing." Artemis held out her hand. "I agree."

"Wait! What if he kills you?" I stayed standing next to the bushes, prepared to grab my bow and arrows if needed.

"He can't kill me. The only thing that can kill us is an apocalyptic vacuum, and the last time we checked on the whereabouts of it, it was a few millennia away." She shrugged. "Don't worry, sweetie. I've won just about every duel we've had."

"Just about isn't good enough." I took the bow and arrows out of the bush and had them ready. Apollo had already known they were there.

"Let's go on the deck, just in case this gets out of hand." Cole took my elbow and led me up the steps. "Let's get this over with. There are things we want to do today."

Apollo and Artemis clasped hands, and the wind picked up around us, blowing my hair in my face. In the time it took me to swipe it out of my eyes, they were a blur across the yard.

One second one of them had the other on the ground and the next they were ten feet in the air, colliding. The ground shook as they landed, the momentum of their bodies creating a hole at least three feet deep and sending dirt and grass flying.

"Looks like I can get my pool now." I hugged Cole's arm. "They started digging for us."

"I just put weed and feed on the lawn," Eli grumbled. "This is ridiculous. They just fight and damage property for five minutes? How will we even know who the winner is?"

"Fuck if I know." Cole put his cheek against the top of my head. "I was thinking tonight we could all get out for a bit."

"Is it safe?" I gasped as my mom took a hard hit and flew halfway across the yard about a hundred feet and then, like nothing had just happened, jumped to her feet and sprinted toward Apollo.

They collided again, the sound of their bodies hitting reminiscent of thunder. I didn't understand how Silas and Xander weren't outside watching this when there was so much noise. But maybe *that* was the problem, the noise.

"How are they even keeping time? I didn't set a timer or anything." Eli looked at his phone. "I think it's been about four minutes."

Apollo snagged Artemis by her hair and swung her around in circles, letting her go and sending her flying into a tree trunk. I started to move forward and Cole pulled me back just as Artemis pushed to her feet and released a battle cry.

They met like two raging bulls in the center of the lawn, moving so fast it was hard to tell what was going on. Did I have the potential to fight like they were? Cole had been working with me on fight skills, but there had to be untapped potential lying dormant inside me. I could feel it.

Both of them stopped like a switch had been flipped and met back in the original spot they had discussed the duel. They clasped hands, both not even breathing hard from their fight.

"One, two, three, four, I declare a thumb war," they said in unison.

"What the actual fuck?" I squeezed the bridge of my nose. "They're deciding our lives with their thumbs."

Cole barked out a laugh and then covered his mouth when I pinned him with a glare. "You're right. Not funny."

It was over in seconds, and Artemis raised her arms in the air in victory. Apollo put his hands on his hips and shook his head in disbelief. And that was it. The duel was over and all our problems solved.

"It's settled. Apollo will leave you alone." Artemis sounded cocky as hell. "If he goes against the contract, he'll spend one hundred years locked in a scorpion filled cave."

"We're going to need a lot of therapy after this is all over." Eli kissed my temple. "I'm going to go do some admin work I've been slacking on."

Eli went inside, leaving me and Cole awkwardly standing on the deck looking down at Artemis and Apollo having some kind of silent conversation with their eyes. I didn't think for one second this was over, but it could wait until after we dealt with OQ.

"Use those arrows wisely." Apollo nodded his chin at me and then disappeared.

"How'd he do that?" Cole stared slack-jawed where Apollo had just been. "Can Ivy do it?"

"We won't know until we try." Artemis looked at the trees. "The deer are calling me."

And with that, she skipped across the yard and vanished into the forest.

I frowned up at Cole, and he swiped some stray hairs from in front of my eyes. "They acted as if it was normal to want to kill another family member... or anyone, for that matter."

"I imagine a few screws are loose." He kissed my forehead. "I told my mom I'd bake with her today." He ran a thumb across my twisted-up lips. "Just give her time. She doesn't do well with change, never has."

"I wish she'd at least give me a chance." I knew the more time she spent with me, the more she'd learn to tolerate me. "I'll just go see what Silas and Xander are up to."

We parted ways, and I went to the art studio, knocking on the door. Silas was still working on something for me, and I was starting to grow impatient.

"Just a second." Silas went silent for a moment. *"Okay, come in with your eyes closed."*

"What if I fall?" I shut my eyes. There were many opportunities I'd had to take a quick peek through their vision, but I'd been a good girlfriend. Now I really wanted to peek.

The door opened, and Xander's scent washed over me. "I'll help you."

He led me in and stopped me, moving away. I heard him grunt as he flopped down on the couch.

"Do I get to see what you've been working on?" I twisted my hands in front of me, not sure what to expect.

What if he'd made a sculpture of my vagina? Was I supposed to smile and act like I loved it?

Silas wrapped his arms around me, resting his chin on my shoulder. His scruff tickled my skin, and I leaned back into him.

"Open them, bunny."

It took my eyes a second to adjust after having them closed, but then they cleared, revealing a hip-high sculpture of a wolf, its head tilted back in a howl.

Tears filled my eyes. He'd salvaged all my mom's china and figurines and used them to cover the sculpture in a kaleidoscope of color.

"You…" I choked on my words and dropped to my knees in front of it, carefully ghosting my fingers over the curves. "It's beautiful and so special. Thank you."

After my house had the explosion, I thought most things were damaged beyond repair. Silas hadn't even told me he'd taken the broken porcelain and china.

"I wanted you to still be able to have the memories." He was behind me and started stroking the top of my head. "It's okay?"

Wiping my tears with the back of my hands, I stood. "Is it okay? It's amazing."

I threw my arms around him and buried my face in his neck. It was the best present I could have asked for.

"There are still some pieces that need to dry and then a protective coating I need to put on." He pulled away and took my chin between his thumb and forefingers. "I love you."

"I love you." I leaned forward and brushed my lips over his.

The sweet kiss quickly turned heated, and he pulled me with him as he walked backward. Our tongues tangled briefly before our lips left each other. He sat down on the couch, pulling me with him; his eyes already half hooded.

Xander looked around awkwardly, and I started to stand.

"Sit." I lowered myself to straddle Silas and reached over to tug Xander toward me. Fisting his shirt, I brought our foreheads together. "I want you to watch."

He licked his lips, his tongue ever so lightly brushing across my lower lip. "And if I want to join?"

"We'll leave that up to Silas." I kissed him, my tongue seeking out his as I slowly began rocking on top of Silas.

Xander groaned against my lips, his head tilting to the side to ravish my mouth deeper. Silas's hands settled on my hips, guiding me up and down his stiff cock. The friction of my jeans with each stroke made my core clench with need.

Pulling away from both men, I stood, taking off my shirt and bra. They watched with rapt attention, their eyes never leaving my tits as I leaned forward and slid my jeans and panties down my legs. Their attention lit a fire in me that could only be extinguished by one of them buried deep inside me.

I stood before them bare, letting them get their fill as I tweaked my nipples until they were hard points. "Take off your clothes."

No time was wasted shucking clothing, and I looked between them, drinking them in like they'd done me. They were glorious, with well-defined muscles and cocks that could have sonnets dedicated to them.

"Get on your knees, bunny." Silas stroked his cock, paying extra attention to the weeping tip. "I want to paint your lips."

Damn. That was hot as hell.

I lowered to the floor, using our discarded clothes under my knees. Taking his cock in my hand, I applied just the right amount of pressure that brought another bead of pre-cum to the tip.

"Look at those pretty pink lips." He wrapped his hand over mine and rubbed his cock against my closed lips. "Do you want to see her lips wrapped around my cock, Xander?"

"More than anything in the world." Xander was backing up toward the couch and I wrapped an arm around his thigh, pulling him close. "Slide your lips around him, baby."

My eyes on Xander's, I slowly opened my mouth, letting Silas inside. Xander's cock twitched as if giving me all the encouragement to continue.

"Sexy as hell with your lips around my cock, taking me to the back of your throat." Silas buried a hand in my hair. "Swallow me."

His cock hit the back of my throat and I swallowed, using a hand to roll his balls in my hand. His eyes rolled back and his mouth opened in pleasure as I swallowed him again and again.

Just as his hips began to roll, I pulled away, moving my mouth to Xander's dick. I licked and sucked at the sensitive flesh underneath before taking him all the way. He moved his hands to his chest where he pinched his nipples.

My core clenched at the sight, and I switched back to Silas, giving him a few hard pulls with my mouth before switching again. Slowly, they inched closer, standing shoulder to shoulder as I alternated between their cocks.

"I need in that pussy of yours." Silas sat down on the couch before I could stop him. "Come here."

Releasing Xander, I stood and sauntered toward Silas. He leaned forward and grabbed my hips, pulling me down on top of him. Our lips met, and I was dizzy with lust as our tongues collided. Reaching between us, I lined him up with my entrance and sank down.

He always hit me in all the right places and I had to stop myself from riding him hard like I tended to do when I was on top. His hands dug into my ass cheeks, controlling my rhythm as I started to move.

A finger trailed down my spine and I clenched around Silas, causing him to rip his lips from mine and let out a feral sound. "Fuck, your pussy was meant for my dick. You know that, right? It's so slick and hot."

His dirty talk when we were together did more for me than I cared to admit.

Lips trailed down my spine as I rocked on top of Silas, making it hard to control myself. With four of them, I never could guess what was going to happen, and this time was no different.

Xander's mouth was on my ass and his tongue traced around Silas's fingers digging into the skin. I was so far gone in sex brain land, I didn't even notice what his trajectory was until he spread my ass cheeks.

"Xander."

"Just getting a better view of your pussy leaving Silas's cock nice and wet." He kissed my other cheek and then let them go.

I was going to combust with both of them talking.

Xander sat back on the couch. "Come here."

Silas helped me move off him and onto Xander. His dick hit me differently, and I groaned into his neck as he rolled his hips under me.

"I want you to lick and suck me clean, bunny." Silas stood on the couch, moving closer so I could take him in my mouth. "Mmm, do you like how good you taste on my cock?"

I hummed my approval around him, causing him to move even lower. His hand went to the back of my head, wrapping my ponytail in his fist. My pussy squeezed around Xander and my orgasm teased up and down my spine.

"I want to see what she tastes like on your cock." Xander had a hand wrapped around the back of Silas's thigh.

"Fuck." Silas's head tipped back with his eyes shut. "Do it."

Xander's lips touched mine as he wrapped them around the side of Silas's base. Silas's legs trembled as I slid him from my mouth and sucked him down the side, the same way Xander was. My lips and tongue occasionally brushed Xander's as we slid up and down Silas's cock in unison.

"I'm going to fucking explode." Silas had both of us by the hair. "I'm going to paint those sexy tits with my cum."

He pulled us both off him, his hand going to his cock and pumping furiously as he orgasmed. His hot cum spilled onto my chest, a growl ripping from his throat.

"Now fuck her until she screams our names." Silas nearly fell off the couch as he sat back down, his chest heaving.

Xander scooted down a little on the couch and began to thrust up in short, hard thrusts. I grabbed the back of the couch. His cock was hitting me in a spot that made my vision swim with tears. His tongue lapped out at a nipple and then took it in his mouth, biting it and sucking it.

"Xander!" My orgasm crashed into me, squeezing him with every muscle and sending him to his own peak.

Silas's hand moved between us, finding my clit and working it into oblivion as I rode out an orgasm that made my tongue go cold.

"Silas!" I threw my head back as my body lit up like all of my nerves were live wires.

I couldn't feel my legs as my body trembled and twitched. I buried my face against Xander's shoulder and laughed.

"Bunny, the last thing a man wants to hear after sex is the woman laughing." His voice was moving away.

Xander trailed his fingers lightly up and down my spine, and if I shut my eyes, I'd probably fall asleep.

"Let's get you cleaned up." Silas helped me stand and then wiped the mess from my chest and between my legs. "You good?"

"I think you two put me in a sex coma." I sat down heavily, my body feeling completely relaxed and satisfied.

If only the rest of my life was like my sex life.

CHAPTER NINE

Ivy

When Artemis said *training*, I thought we'd be working on my fighting skills and using any special abilities I might have. What I didn't expect was to be sitting in the middle of a clearing, deer surrounding me, focusing on finding my inner strength.

We'd been at it for an hour already, and I was having a hard time seeing what the point of the training was. I opened my eyes briefly to see if she was even still there.

She was so quiet, I couldn't even hear her breathe. A serene look was on her face, and I marveled at the fact that she was my mother.

She looked like she could be my sister.

"Focus, youngling. It takes many hours to find the

strength that lies within." Her soothing voice infiltrated my mind. "Shut your eyes and let everything else melt away."

I'd tried. I'd tried so hard not to think about all the wolves locked away somewhere or what the OQ was up to. I'd tried not to think about how much danger my mates were always in. And I definitely tried hard not to think about them giving me orgasms.

I shut my eyes and focused on breathing. This was why I didn't like yoga.

"Why do you think I didn't shift until I was older?" Finding my inner peace also meant tons of unanswered questions flitting through my mind.

"Hm. If I had to guess, it was probably because your wolf wasn't strong enough. What happened to cause you to shift?"

I told her all about how Cole and I had been in a car accident. Originally, I had thought it had something to do with my birthday, but now I wasn't so sure.

"You're half goddess, which means you can still be injured severely, and it would require all of your resources to go toward healing. It's possible that's the only opportunity your wolf had to take a strong enough hold to push forward."

"But I don't have any issues now with shifting."

"Of course not. Your wolf destroyed whatever was keeping her locked away." She made a humming noise. "Now, back to focusing on our inner strength."

It was going to be a long afternoon.

Despite feeling like I hadn't done a damn thing besides sit in a field and soak up the delicious sun, my muscles ached like I'd had a workout. After taking a short power nap and a shower, I joined the guys in the living room, where they were quietly talking.

We were having a date night, and as excited as I was, my nerves were also twisted. Last time we'd gone out to have a good time, three of them had been taken.

"We don't have to go anywhere, you know." Cole turned around on the couch and whistled his approval. "Damn, you look good enough to eat. We should cancel our plans."

I looked down at my knee-length sundress and sandals. "It's just a dress."

"Yes, but..." Eli stood and grabbed me around the waist. "...there's something about a girl in a sundress. The way the light hits and filters through the skirt."

I rolled my eyes and batted him away as he nuzzled into my neck. "Are sundresses the female equivalent of gray sweatpants?"

Silas stood, clicking off the television. "That would be yoga pants."

"Maybe the equivalent of rolled-up shirt sleeves?" Xander jumped to his feet. "We should go if we want to be on time for our reservation."

Butterflies erupted in my stomach and I had no clue why. These men had seen me at my worst and naked on several occasions, but going on a date to a fancy restaurant made me nervous.

We piled into Cole's truck and drove into town. It was weird being back in Arbor Falls after being away for so long. There were a few new restaurants and businesses that had moved into the downtown area, and with the nice weather, people were enjoying the outdoor seating.

"This place is supposed to have the best steaks." Cole pulled into the parking lot.

"Better than Eli's?" Silas reached under the seat and pulled out a case that had a gun. When he saw me staring, he gave me a tight smile. "We have to be prepared."

"I know. I just wish we didn't have to be." I wouldn't be carrying anything, but the rest of them would be.

Cole opened the back door and gave me his hand. "Let's try to not think about anything besides us tonight."

It was easier said than done, but I'd try.

The restaurant was fancier than I expected, with waitstaff dressed in suits. The ambience was romantic with soft lighting.

The hostess led us to a back booth that was big enough to fit eight people. I slid onto the leather seat with two men on each side of me.

"Are we celebrating anything special tonight?" The hostess handed out menus.

"Our girlfriend's birthday." Silas smirked when I glared at him.

The woman looked around the table and raised an eyebrow at me. "You have four boyfriends?"

"Yup." I smiled as her eyes widened.

"Good for you." She seemed to mean that, which made me relax. People could be judgmental as hell when it came to sexuality.

She left us to our menus, and an awkward silence filled the table. I peeked up through my eyelashes to find Cole mouthing something to Eli.

"What's going on?" I shut my menu, already knowing what I wanted to order.

"Uh." Cole picked up his water and took a gulp. "I couldn't remember if I locked the door."

He was lying, but I shrugged. "Who's going to break into our house?"

"You never know these days. Better to always lock the doors." Silas put his hand on my thigh. "What are you getting?"

The mood returned to normal, but I still wasn't convinced. Weird looks were exchanged several times throughout the appetizer. It was driving me nuts. It was almost as if they were nervous about something.

"Is something wrong?" I stabbed a crouton in my salad. "Is it because I called you my boyfriends?"

That was the only thing I could possibly think of that might have caused them all to freak out. But it wasn't like I hadn't referred to them as my boyfriends before... just not out in public.

"We're just not sure if you're going to like part two of our date." Eli put his fork down. "Pretty sure we'll all be sleeping on the couch tonight."

"There's a part two?" I smiled as the waitress put my steak in front of me. The steak was the best in town, and I'd tried just about every restaurant. "I told you guys that I'm easy to please."

"Oh, we know that." Xander winked at me. "I say we skip part two and go straight to part three."

"How many parts are there?" I bit into my steak and groaned. "Fuck, this is so good."

"Well, now there might be four parts," Silas muttered as he adjusted himself under the table. "I love the sounds you make when you put meat in your mouth."

I nearly choked on the piece of steak in my mouth. After taking a drink of water, I cleared my throat. "Will part four involve meat in my mouth?"

"If that's what you want, it can be arranged." Cole grinned, his smile lighting up his entire face.

It was rare now to see any of us with a light in our eyes, and it made my chest constrict. None of us deserved what we'd been through, but it was moments like these that made me have hope for our future.

After devouring appetizers and my dinner, I was more than ready for a nap. My mates had different plans.

"Ready for part two of our date?" We'd just left the restaurant and Eli took one of my hands and Xander the other as we walked down the street, away from where we'd parked.

I looked back over my shoulder to find Cole and Silas with their heads together, discussing something. I strained to hear them, but couldn't hear a thing. "If you guys are planning on how to get me to do anal, my answer will always be no."

Silas snorted. "You brought it up. That must mean it's on your mind."

"How about this... I'll do it when you and Cole do it."

I cackled when they both scrunched up their noses. "That's what I thought."

"It's amazing. I think if we prepped you three with some butt plugs or some thinner dildos, you'd find it's easier to take a cock." Xander was explaining right as we passed by an outdoor dining area and several people looked up in disgust.

I was laughing so hard my stomach hurt as we continued down the street. Talking about anal sex in public probably wasn't the best conversation choice.

We rounded a corner and Xander let my hand go and rushed forward to open a door. "This was Cole's idea by the way."

"Stark Dance?" I stopped in my tracks. "I have two left feet."

"Oh, come on, you aren't that bad." Eli pulled on my hand. "You haven't seen Cole dance yet."

"I'm horrible. Figured this class might help me keep up with Eli and Xander."

"Hey, just because I can hump the ground doesn't mean I can Cha Cha or whatever it is we're doing." Xander followed us into a lobby that was closed off from where I assumed the dance studio was.

"Hi! Welcome to Stark Dance. What can I do for you folks?" The very nice older man behind the counter stood from his chair.

"I signed us up for a class." Cole rubbed his chin. "Heating Up with the Cha Cha is what it was called, I think."

The man looked us up and down. "You're kind of

overdressed. But let me just check to make sure you're in the system."

He sat back down and clicked around. "What's the name?"

"Delaney."

"Ah, yes. Your payment did go through. Now, you are aware that tonight is a special night, correct? The email confirmation should have said it."

"A special night?" Cole leaned on the counter. "I don't recall. Do we need to reschedule?"

"Oh no, not at all. We just like our students to know when our seniors will be in because some don't like seeing them, that's all." The man grinned. "But if you folks are okay with it, then head on down the hall to Studio A."

I was confused about why anyone would have issues with seniors dancing, but nothing really surprised me anymore.

We headed down the hall and entered Studio A, where there was already a large group of senior citizens gathered around chatting.

The man at the receptionist desk was right; we were overdressed. Most of the attendees had on workout attire or loose-fitting clothing.

The conversation practically stopped as we walked in and found a space along one of the mirrored walls to wait.

"Wherever they're dancing, I want to be right behind them."

"Bea, you know that's not appropriate! We don't want to make them uncomfortable."

"Do you think the blonde one is single?"

"I think they are together. All of them. Sweet Jesus."

Cole was pressing his lips together, a laugh threatening to burst free. These seniors had no filter.

A man dressed in a silk robe came into the studio and sauntered over to where a laptop was on top of a large speaker. "All right, ladies and gentlemen! Are you ready for it to get hot in here?"

Cheers went up around the room and all the groups that were standing around the perimeter moved further out on the dance floor, partnering up.

The next fifteen minutes was what I would have expected from a normal dance class. We were taught the basic steps and switched off in our little group.

I had thought it was strange at first that the man was wearing a robe, but it was probably a dress. Fashion was always changing, and a man wearing a dress wasn't something new.

The music cut off, and the man clapped his hands together to get everyone's attention. Despite my initial hesitancy about dancing, I was having a lot of fun. I'd only stepped on each of the guys' feet once or twice, and we'd done nothing but laugh and joke around the entire time.

"Now that we're warmed up, I'm going to dim the lights and let you get more comfortable. As always, do what you're comfortable with."

And then he took off his robe.

I was so shocked at the nude man standing right in front of thirty or so people, that I couldn't even look away.

"Um, Cole." Eli slowly looked around the room. "They're getting naked."

"Oh my God." Silas covered his mouth so his laugh didn't fill the room. "What is this?"

The music was turned back on and people started dancing. Naked.

Xander put his hand on Cole's shoulder. "Didn't know you had a thing for wrinkles."

"I-" Cole's face turned bright red, and he ran his hand down his face. "The website and email didn't say anything about this, I swear."

"Is there a problem over here?" the instructor, Julius, asked, dancing his way over to us. *Everything* did the Cha Cha right along with him. I was dying on the inside, trying to stop myself from laughing.

"We didn't know this was a nude dance class." Eli avoided eye contact. "Would it be okay if we showed ourselves the way out?"

"What? I'm staying." Silas was grinning ear to ear and unbuttoned his pants. "I've always wanted to join a nudist colony; this is a good first step."

I grabbed his hand, my giggle escaping despite my best efforts to keep it in.

"You are free to leave. The class description and email did include information that attire was optional."

"I thought that meant dance clothing." Cole was spluttering, and I couldn't blame him. None of us were ever going to let him forget this.

The man laughed and patted Cole's arm, leaving his hand there. "You should stay. Become free of the socially constructed confines of clothing. This class is all about loving yourself and being comfortable in your own skin."

Cole looked to Eli for help, but Eli shrugged. "We'll go. Thank you for everything."

"Any time." After another pat, Julius danced his way back to the front of the room and we got the hell out of there.

~

"Did you see how red his face got? It matched your hair." Silas had not stopped since we stumbled out of the dance studio laughing our asses off. "It's a shame we couldn't stay."

"Shut up," Cole grumbled from behind us.

I let go of Xander's hand and slowed down to walk next to Cole. "I don't think I've ever laughed so hard in my life."

"Well, I'm glad I can amuse you all. Tonight was supposed to be special, and I ruined it." It was unlike Cole to sulk or throw a pity party, so I pulled him to a stop.

"It was perfect. Don't beat yourself up over wrinkly balls, all right?" I grinned up at him and he groaned. "We're all having a good time, that's what matters."

"You're right. Life is too short to fret over wrinkly scrotums." He snorted a laugh, his eyes twinkling. "Time for part three."

"We're doing something else?" I was excited. Despite my earlier feelings, I realized I had nothing to worry about. It didn't matter where we were or what we were doing, these men loved me.

"We just have a short drive." He kissed me gently.

"There shouldn't be any naked old people where we're going next." Xander piped up from where the other three were waiting for us.

"Damn it." Cole groaned, linking his arm with mine. "I'm never going to hear the end of it, am I?"

"Nope," we all said in unison as we climbed into the truck giggles still escaping.

Twenty minutes later we were driving down a dark road lined with trees. It was a few miles before our regular turn to get to the house and my curiosity was piqued.

They had gotten weird again. Cole and Eli had gone quiet, but Xander and Silas were nonstop talking about some fight that had been on television the night before.

I watched out the window, reminding myself that they weren't taking me to the middle of nowhere to kill me. The intrusive thoughts were unwarranted, but after everything we'd been through, would it be such a stretch?

Tears welled in my eyes as guilt filled me. Here these four men were giving me all the attention in the world, loving me with all their hearts, and I was imagining them deceiving me.

"What's wrong?" Eli's hand rubbed my knee.

"Nothing." I smiled at him. "I guess I'm just tired."

I could tell from the look on his face that he didn't believe me one bit. "We're almost there."

"Where are we going? It's in our territory?" I looked

back out the window as we continued to wind our way through dense trees.

"It's on the line where west and east used to be separated." Silas turned around and gave me a sheepish smile.

What was going on?

"Shut your eyes," Eli whispered in my ear. "And no peeking through us."

"You guys aren't going to kill me, are you?" I laughed, even though my stomach was doing somersaults. At least I hoped that was why my stomach was flopping all over the place.

"Of course not. Shut them."

A few minutes passed of bumping along the gravel road until the truck came to a stop and Cole turned off the engine.

"Keep them closed until we tell you to open them." Eli still had his hand on my knee and only removed it once my door was opened.

"I'm going to lift you out." Cole wrapped me in his arms and lifted me out of the truck.

The doors shut, and I could feel them standing around me.

"Open them."

CHAPTER TEN

Cole

My entire world changed the moment Ivy walked into it. I'd never realized what it meant to truly love someone until her.

When Xander made a comment to me a few weeks ago about the backyard making him sick to his stomach, I had an idea. An idea that would help us all start over… together.

Ivy opened her eyes and gasped.

Laid out on an empty plot of land amongst the trees were lights outlining where the foundation of a new house would be built.

She walked forward, closer to where we'd decided the front door would be, a welcome mat where it would soon be.

She raised a shaking hand to her face but didn't say anything.

We'd all been nervous about her reaction to it. She'd moved a lot in the last year, and there we were planning another move.

We followed her as she stepped over the lights and headed for the two air mattresses we'd set up where the bedroom would be. It overlooked a pond the size of a football field.

"Maybe we should start drinking this now." Silas held up the small cooler we'd stashed a few bottles of champagne in.

"What is this?" She finally turned, tears in her eyes.

"Well, if you want, this is where our new house is going to be built." I took a deep breath, bracing myself for her to say it was too much too soon. Living together in my house was one thing, but building one together was a whole other level of commitment.

"It has a pond." Eli's arm brushed mine as he stood next to me. "We know you wanted a pool."

"You don't have to do this. I love your house." She came back toward us, a soft smile on her lips that made my stomach flip.

"I want this to be our house." I took her hands. "All of ours, not just mine."

Xander stood behind her, kissing her shoulder. "Say yes."

"Yes." She threw her arms around my neck and kissed me. "A million times yes."

She moved on to the others and was beaming.

"Let's get comfy and have some celebratory drinks."

Eli took her hand and led her to the air mattresses. "We were thinking this could be where our bedroom is upstairs with a large skylight to look at the stars and French doors leading out to a balcony overlooking the pond."

Xander followed right behind them while I stayed back, watching my family. Damn. I would never have imagined that I'd also gain three best friends.

"Are you going to cry, Coco?" Silas bumped into my shoulder. I admit, I got a little misty-eyed there for a minute.

"I'm not going to cry." Our shoulders pressed together, and I sighed. "Things are weird now."

"What do you mean?" Silas set the cooler at his feet.

"You won't meet my eye." I looked over at him staring straight ahead. "I shouldn't have pushed you to do anything with me."

He shrugged. "You didn't. It's just... when you're with women your whole life and then let a man touch you, and enjoy it? I don't know what to do with how I feel."

"How do you feel?"

"Unsure... worried. I know Ivy says she's okay with it, but what if a year down the road we're all fucking each other and she suddenly decides she doesn't want us all... together."

"Is that really what you're worried about?" I took his hand, and he sucked in a breath so hard I wondered if it had hurt. "Or is it because you don't know what to do with your feelings toward us?"

He didn't pull away, so I kept his hand in mine. It

was comforting to feel his skin against mine. I couldn't explain it, and it didn't necessarily need an explanation.

"It's because I'm scared of loving four people and losing all of them." There was so much pain in his voice I was taken aback. "Everyone I have loved has left me. My mom, my dad, Mama, Pops."

My lips twitched watching Xander tackle Ivy onto the air mattress, drawing a shriek and then giggles from her.

"I know it hurts to lose people you love, but doesn't it hurt more not to let yourself love and be loved?" I looked down at our hands. "Did I think I'd be entertaining the idea of being with other men? No. Does it scare the fuck out of me? Sure. But it feels right, like we are exactly where we need to be… with each other."

Silas's own smile flashed across his face as we watched Eli jump on the air mattress next to Xander and Ivy and send them bouncing. "You seem *too* okay with it for it just now being an epiphany."

"It felt amazing, didn't it?" The memory of the three of us together made my cock tingle with awareness. "I'm not asking to fuck your ass."

Silas laughed and let go of my hand and shoved me away before picking up the cooler. "Good, because I'm going to fuck yours first."

"Are you two going to stand over there all night or are you going to bring the drinks?" Xander shouted.

"We good?" I took the cooler from him.

"We're good." Silas suddenly wrapped his arms around me. "Thanks for being a great friend… who sometimes grabs my dick."

I laughed, shoving him away from me and heading for the wrestling match that was happening on the air mattresses. Eli had suggested we bring the mattresses from the guest rooms, and I'd shot that idea down. It might have been okay with tarps underneath. Then I wouldn't have to flinch every time someone was slammed down onto it.

~

THE NIGHT HAD BEEN PERFECT. After polishing off the two bottles of champagne, which surprisingly got all of us a little tipsy, we laid on the mattresses, watching the stars.

We hadn't planned on spending the night, but Silas, Eli, and Xander were already passed out.

"What did you and Silas talk about earlier?" Ivy had moved next to me, using my chest as her pillow.

"Feelings." I absently twirled her hair around my finger. "It's one thing to fool around with each other, but I think it's a lot more than that."

"It seems only natural. We've all been through a lot together." She rolled to her side and traced a finger along my jaw. "We're all connected, bound by a force we can't see."

"Is that what Artemis told you?" I closed my eyes as her fingers explored my face.

"No. I saw it."

I raised my eyebrows, and she laughed softly. "During my training earlier, which was more of mediation and looking inside myself for my inner strength. I only felt it for a few seconds, but my connection to you four is more of a web of connections. They exist between you guys too. Stronger between Eli and Xander, but there for all of you."

"I'm just going with what feels right." I kissed her temple.

"I want you all to be just as happy as I am." She played with a button on my shirt. "Maybe now Silas will stop trying to get me to try anal."

I buried my face in her hair, trying to laugh quietly. "He'll never stop because there's the off chance that one day you'll say yes."

"I'll try it the day you both do." She patted my stomach. "So lube up, baby."

"I should get this in writing. I mean… it does look like it feels good once the initial breach happens. I just have to convince Silas."

"Breach?" She snorted on a laugh. "I think I like invasion better."

My hand found her thigh, and I ran my fingertips across her smooth skin. She shivered and her skin broke out in goosebumps. "My fingers want to do some invading right about now."

"We'll wake them up." She sucked in a breath as I moved my fingers to her inner thigh. She needed to wear dresses and skirts more often; it made access that much easier.

"If they haven't woken up already, they aren't going to. How quiet can you be?" I licked her neck as I trailed a finger along her panties. "Let me take care of you."

Her eyes shut and her lips parted as I pushed my

finger against her panties. They were already wet, and I grinned against her skin. I loved how responsive she was to our touch.

I pulled her panties to the side, and she gasped as I teased her entrance. She was slick with need and I was half tempted to use my dick instead.

"Stop teasing." She rolled her hips up, trying to get me inside.

Instead of complying, I ran my finger up to her clit, circling it a few times before moving back to her entrance. I slowly pushed inside her, not because she needed me to go slow, but because I wanted to drive her crazy.

I brushed my lips across her ear, and she shuddered as my breath fanned across her skin. "I love how hot and wet you are for me. I want you to come all over my hand."

She made a small whimper, her hips chasing my finger every time I pulled it out. I slid two in and she groaned softly.

"Are you thinking about how bad you want my cock buried inside you?"

"Yes."

I pushed another finger in. "I'm thinking about how good it feels when Silas slides his cock in right next to mine."

She whimpered as my other hand descended on her clit, working it at the same pace as my fingers. I was honestly surprised we were quiet enough not to wake anyone up.

"Come for me, baby." I worked my hands faster,

pressing my mouth to hers to stifle the sounds of her release as she clenched around my fingers.

Her body trembled as she came down from her high, and I pulled my fingers from her.

"Take my dick out. I want you to watch me jack myself off with your cum."

As soon as my dick was free, I wrapped my hand around myself and began working my cock. I was already on the edge and it didn't take long before my own release covered my hand.

"You didn't think this through very well." Ivy sat up and looked around for what I could only assume was something to clean us both up with.

"I'll see if I have something in the truck." I carefully shimmied off the air mattress and went to find some napkins in my center console.

When I got back, Ivy was already fast asleep, and I was left with a giant grin on my face.

～

THE NEXT DAY, our focus turned to finding the OQ. Trevor gave no indication that the coalition was moving toward rescuing the wolves.

My dad and Eli's dad both agreed with our decision to locate the threat on our own. There were enough of us that we're willing to risk the wrath of the coalition to do what was right.

"I just got a call back. There are only two places that have that quantity of dog food delivered. One is a rescue organization. The other is a storage facility where they are directed to put the food in an unlocked unit." Eli pulled up an overhead picture of the storage facility. "Sara is trying to access their security footage."

"How long is that going to take?" Silas leaned back in his chair and put his hand behind his head. "How often are the deliveries?"

"Once a week. The thing is, we don't have any clue when they retrieve it and the invoices say to wait for a text the morning of delivery for the unit to drop it off."

"We'd have to watch a week's worth of security footage."

"Nope." Sara looked up from her laptop. "They only have a camera at the entrance. It's a pretty cheap place."

"So now what?" Silas let out a frustrated grunt as he let the front legs of his chair slam back down on the floor. "We're going to watch the videos and look for any weird dudes in moving trucks?"

"I fast-forwarded through just a day's worth of footage and there were over fifty vehicles that went in and out." Sara closed her laptop. "The best option is to stake out the facility. It's going to be noticeable that they're loading up fifty-pound bags of dog food and we have a rough idea of what size unit they need."

"That sounds painful. The storage place wouldn't give you any information? What about their invoices?"

"They told me they had no clue what people kept in their storage lockers. Their invoices aren't digital."

"One of us could shift and see if we can smell it. It's worth a shot, anyway." Eli pulled up another picture that was the blueprint map of the sizes of the storage units. He'd circled all the possibilities. "They're delivering tomorrow at ten in the morning. We can go and rent a unit ourselves so we have an excuse to be there."

"Are we going to include Ivy in this?" Sara crossed her arms over her chest. "She's not going to be happy if you don't."

"Someone needs to stay here with Xander." Eli closed his laptop and crossed his arms on the top. "The more of us that are there, the riskier it is."

"He's right. We'll tell her we're going and what we're doing."

"Manny and I will stay with Xander. Manny is not scheduled tomorrow." Sara smiled broadly. "Now your problem is solved."

~

OUR PROBLEM WAS NOT, in fact, solved. Xander refused to stay behind, but he agreed to stay inside a vehicle where he couldn't be seen. We were all adults, so trying to stop him was futile.

We'd decided to take two cars since it would be less suspicious with the five of us. We'd also be able to cover more ground. I wasn't fond of the idea of splitting up, but we should be safe if we didn't make any rash decisions.

Ivy came out of her closet and spun around. "Does this outfit say we're moving?"

She was in ripped jeans and a faded volleyball shirt. I wanted to rip it all off and throw her on the bed, but we needed to leave soon.

"It's passable." I put down one of her books I'd been

flipping through and stood. "I wish you'd change your mind about coming. If you did, I bet Xander would decide to stay behind too."

She sat on the end of the bed and put on a shoe. "When we separate, bad things happen. There's strength in numbers."

"Yeah, but instead of something bad happening to three of us, it will happen to all of us." I went to her dresser and looked at the pictures lining the top. "Any word from Riley?"

"She's texted me a few times to check in." She sighed as she tied her shoes. "I hope when the baby is born they don't have to stay away. I want to love all up on him and then promptly give him back."

I scratched my beard and turned to look at her. It wasn't the first time she had hinted that babies weren't her thing, but I didn't want to ask if she was trying to tell us she didn't want kids at all. "Him?"

"With all that big dick energy, it's going to be a boy." She bent at the waist and did some kind of magic trick to get her hair in a bun.

"What would you know about them having big dick energy? Do you and Riley talk about dicks or have you seen theirs?" I put my hands on my hips in mock anger.

She rolled her eyes. "You don't talk about me with the guys?"

"Ah, well... that's different. We're your boyfriends. They're not." I grabbed her hips and pulled her to me. "If you need to be reminded of the only big dick energy you should be thinking about..."

"How do you feel about penis piercings?" She was

going for shock value now, and I was sure my shock showed because she threw her head back and laughed.

"One of them has a pierced dick?" I covered my crotch. "How does that not hurt?"

"What have I walked into?" Silas was standing in the doorway, looking a little pale.

"Ivy was sharing how she talks about our dicks with her best friend." I kissed her nose and headed for the door. "We should get going. It's a two-and-a-half-hour drive."

As I walked down the stairs I heard Silas ask, "Have you told her my dick is the biggest?"

He wished.

CHAPTER ELEVEN

Ivy

The scenery whizzed past us as we drove along the highway. We were finally making progress on taking down OQ so we never had to worry about them again. I couldn't wait for all the drama to be behind us and to finally settle in with my men.

I was already making a list in my head of things I wanted in the new house. It was a nice distraction from all the what ifs that constantly flooded my brain.

Eli reached across the console of the SUV and put his hand on my thigh. "You all right over there?"

Putting my hand over his, I smiled. "Just ready to get this over and done with. Sometimes it doesn't feel real."

"Tell me about it," he muttered. "Sometimes when I wake up in the morning, I don't want to get out of bed."

"I didn't know you were feeling that way." I turned in my seat. "You can always come talk to me."

Eli looked in the rearview mirror at Xander listening to music in the back. He said he was fine coming along with us, he'd immediately put in headphones and hadn't said a word since we'd left.

"Everyone had enough to deal with." He shrugged. "I'll be fine once all of this is over."

"After we find out where they have the wolves, we should get Artemis to help." I looked back out the window as we crossed over a river. "She's a little crazy, but I don't think she can die."

"And what about you?"

I hadn't exactly talked to them about my lifespan potential, although I did tell Silas about becoming part tree to extend his life. He'd laughed and said the only part of him that was like a tree was his dick.

Once things calmed down, I'd urge him to explore that side of himself. It might not have been the coolest thing, but it might provide some level of protection.

"I'd have to take steps to prolong my life." He squeezed my leg as I bounced it a bit at the thought of being asleep for months or years at a time. "I'd have to go into stasis like they do."

"Is that something you're considering?" God, he sounded sad. I wanted to tell him to pull the SUV over so I could give him a hug, but we were just about to our destination.

"Not in a million years. I have everything I could ever want. Why would I want to watch my loved ones be taken away from me and continue on with my life for eternity?" It was depressing to think about, now that I was actually running the idea through my head. "No wonder Edward was such an asshole about it to Bella."

"Oh, geez." Eli chuckled. "You're one of those girls."

"Those are fighting words, Eli. I think that deserves a spanking."

Turning off the highway, the GPS alerted us we were less than a mile away. Once we found the storage unit the delivery was made to, we had a few different plans depending on what we encountered.

We got to the storage facility and went into the front office to rent a storage unit. We were going to try to appear as inconspicuous as possible by moving empty boxes in and out. Cole and Silas had arrived ten minutes before us, so it wouldn't seem like we were together.

We got back to the SUV to find Xander was no longer in the backseat.

"Xander? Where the fuck did you go?" I couldn't keep the panic out of our connection. So much had happened already, and the last thing we needed was for Xander to lose it when we were hours away from home.

"I wanted to have a look around. I'll come find you guys when I'm done."

Have a look around? We'd already done a good enough look around on Google Earth. Next to the storage facility was an empty field that hadn't been weeded in at least a year, on the other side was the street, and behind it was a mechanic shop. There was nothing suspicious about any of those things.

"Should we drag him back to the car?" I put my hands on my hips and looked around, trying to find him. "I know he's an adult, but sometimes you guys need a firm hand."

I wasn't trying to be funny, but Eli started laughing anyway. "Let's just leave him. He'll be fine. He wouldn't have come if he didn't feel like he was mentally prepared to do this." Eli went around to the passenger side and opened my door. "Now you'll have two asses to put a firm hand on."

The last thing I should have been thinking about was spanking their asses, but for some reason, the thought excited me and distracted me from the nervousness I felt. I was supposed to be the alpha, but that didn't mean the alpha couldn't get scared or nervous.

We drove down the center row of the facility to the back and parked in front of our unit. The trunk area of the SUV was loaded with empty boxes. As long as no one else was nearby, we would just keep loading and unloading them.

"Are you guys in position?" I asked Cole and Silas. The plan for them was the same, except they had a view of the entrance.

"Yup. Hopefully, we see the truck come in, so we don't have to hunt around to the different units to find it," Cole replied.

"Keep an eye out for Xander. He said he wanted to look around a bit."

"Got it, Alpha."

Something about having Cole call me *Alpha* did something inside of me. He'd been dealing with the role change pretty well lately. But I also thought he'd been different since almost dying for a second time.

He'd seemed more carefree and playful since the arrow incident. But even before that, he'd mellowed out considerably since I met him. As much as he said he loved being alpha, the pressure was immense.

Besides making sure our territory was safe, I also had to deal with wolves who were making bad choices that might potentially lead to exposure, and stay in contact with other packs so, if things went wrong, we'd have allies.

It really was a full-time job, especially now with everything going on with the OQ.

"This is a decent size storage unit. I bet this is the size they're delivering the dog food to." Eli had just rolled up the door and was staring inside the empty space. "You know, I read somewhere that there are some people who run businesses out of their storage unit. They keep merchandise inside or they even run the whole production from it." He popped open the trunk and grabbed a box. "It would get kind of hot, though, and it's not like these things have air conditioners. I think you can rent ones that are climate-controlled if you need to. That's probably hella expensive."

I blinked at him. His rambling about storage units was endearing but also concerning. "There might be electrical outlets or people could plug things into their cars." I grabbed a box too and carried it like it was heavy. "Are you all right?"

"I'm fine. Why?" He gave me a funny look.

"You're rambling about climate-controlled storage units." Putting the empty box down, I turned to find him leaning against the side of the SUV, watching me. "What?"

"I still don't understand why the coalition is waiting to make their move."

"Your guess is as good as mine. I think anything run by Apollo needs to be questioned. He had a psychopath at the head of his operations." I quickly looked around, hoping Xander hadn't snuck up on us. "Xander really hasn't talked about that night. Neither have you."

He walked back into the unit, grabbing me around the waist. "There's nothing to talk about."

"It's okay if this whole thing makes you nervous. I think we're all a bit nervous about what might happen." I wrapped my arms around him. "I'm worried about Xander."

"We all are. I've tried talking to him when the timing was right, and he completely shut down." Eli stroked my back, and I wanted to shut my eyes. "He's shared a lot of himself in a short period. We need to give him more time and space to deal with all of this."

I knew he was right, but it didn't stop me from wanting to check in on Xander every ten minutes. I felt like he was going to slip away and we'd never get him back. I needed all of my men, not just three of them.

"The delivery truck is here." Xander sounded distant, like he was on the cusp of being out of range.

I didn't like it.

We'd been testing our ability to communicate with each other, and it seemed like the defining feature was that I had to be present and in the same general vicinity. Our range of communication was wider if we were around our own pack, the connections between us all helping move the message along to its intended target. It was an interesting phenomenon that I really wanted to know more about.

After the shitstorm that was upon us was over, I'd have time to research it more. There were a lot of special projects I was already planning when all was said and done. I couldn't wait to design the new house, start a fire prevention program, and put more things in place as a pack to reduce our carbon footprint.

Plus, I was about to be an aunt.

I knew the guys all wanted to have babies, but I just couldn't imagine myself with one of my own. It never bothered me until one of them brought it up or hinted at it with something they would say or do. I might feel differently in a couple years, but right then, I wasn't keen on the thought of being pregnant.

"The truck turned down the last row." Silas interrupted my thoughts, and I kicked myself for getting distracted.

"Do you think we should walk over there and take a look?" Being stealthy was something new to me.

"Cole and Silas have that part covered." Eli grabbed another box and took it in to the storage unit. "We should have brought a deck of cards or something. We could be here for a while."

I dropped my own box on top of his and wrapped

my arms around his neck. "We can make out like horny teenagers in the backseat."

A flash of red dropped from the front of the storage unit and a naked woman with flaming red hair was standing in front of us. She didn't seem to care that it was broad daylight and that the only thing blocking her from view was the SUV.

"I'm afraid this party is over." Deer on a cracker. She even sounded like me. "Get in your vehicle and vacate the premises."

"And you are?" I knew exactly who she was, but I wanted to hear it from her. I didn't exactly know if she was a threat or not. All signs pointed to yes, but my wolf wasn't responding to her at all.

"I'm here on behalf of the coalition. You're interfering with an investigation of utmost importance." She sounded like she had been fed the lines to repeat. Maybe she was brainwashed.

"The coalition isn't exactly trustworthy." Eli took a step forward and put himself slightly in front of me. I appreciated the gesture and put my hand on his arm.

The woman's green eyes dropped to my hand on his arm and then looked back up at me. "The OQ gets sloppy when they think no one is onto them. They've become more and more lax over the last week." She put her hand on her hip and moved farther into the storage unit, closer to us. "Look, I know that you want to help save the wolves. I do too, but you can't just take five people in there and expect to have a good outcome. There needs to be a coordinated effort with the trained agents. I don't know what Trevor has told you, but there are hundreds of agents working on this. You guys are jeopardizing all the work that has been done."

"You've been inside." What was Eli talking about? "Do you think the coalition should wait to make a move after what you've seen?"

Sadness crossed her face. "The coalition will take action soon."

"You didn't answer my question."

"If it were me running it? No. I wouldn't wait. The longer those wolves are trained, the worse they get." She shuddered. "I don't know how they're going to come back from the things those people have made them do."

"How are they doing it?" I was trying to wrap my head around the fact that she'd been in the place where all the wolves were kept.

"Before they bring them to the main warehouse, they have training centers where they find the strongest wolves to put all the other wolves in their place. Then they condition the wolves to think that a whistle is the one controlling them instead of the stronger wolves."

Eli tensed, and I rubbed his arm. "They control them with a whistle?"

"It's a very specific frequency. I've never heard anything else like it." She looked over her shoulder. "I need to go before I'm spotted. Get yourselves out of here."

"Wait! What's your name? We should get coffee or something sometime." She seemed sane, and my whole reason for moving in the first place was to find my biological family.

A small smile spread across her face. "I'm Wren, and I'd love to get coffee sometime, but as soon as this job is done, I'm being sent on another special assignment deep undercover. I'm not sure how long I'll be gone."

And with that, she shifted and scurried away, the white tip of her tail the last thing we saw of her.

CHAPTER TWELVE

Eli

The coalition had known all along what we were up to, yet they'd waited until we'd gotten all the way to the storage facility to tell us to back off. It made no sense. I didn't know what kind of games they were playing, but there were hundreds of lives on the line. We didn't have time for games.

"Do you think we can trust her?" Ivy walked to the opening of the unit and looked out. "She completely disappeared."

"I think anyone that works for the coalition or is a descendent of Apollo needs to be handled with care." I went and stood next to her. "Why let us get all the way here if they knew we were coming here in the first place?"

Ivy shrugged. "Maybe they didn't know for sure."

"Oh, they knew for sure. They probably know exactly what time the OQ comes to get the dog food, too. They probably let us come because they aren't coming for a while." I went to the SUV and got my small toolkit out. "We're still going to put the tracker in the food."

I was done playing games. At the end of the day, I was going to have to live with myself if something happened to the wolves and we did nothing.

"Hey, we have a problem." Silas sounded unsure if he should panic or not.

"Is it Xander?"

"No. It's the redhead with a bushy tail who just scared the crap out of me." I could almost see Silas running his hand down his face. *"She said to pack up and go."*

"Yeah, she came over here too. I'm still going to put the tracker in the dog food." I didn't care if she was more than likely still watching us. Let her report back to the coalition. It wasn't like they were currently in contact with us, anyway. Perhaps this would speed up that process.

"The truck is leaving. Now is our window of opportunity. Last row to the east."

We walked quickly without looking too suspicious to the row where they had directed. Silas was already standing at the other end, looking around the corner. *"It's number forty-two."*

His head disappeared back around the corner, and Ivy stayed at the end where we were to keep watch. I jogged to the unit, looking around to see if there were any cameras. Everything looked clear. They changed units every delivery, so I was fairly confident there weren't any.

The lock was a combination type, but even those were easy to pick. It popped open with ease, and I rolled up the door partway and ducked underneath. There were two pallets, and I quickly went to the first one, made a tiny incision in a bag, and put the small tracker inside. I dabbed some superglue over the hole and then I was back outside, locking the door in under a minute.

"Tracker is in place. Let's get out of here."

I walked quickly down the aisle, grabbing Ivy's hand and going back toward the SUV. As we drew closer, I saw there was a man leaning against the front end. Apollo.

Shit. He was the last person we needed to deal with.

"Apollo's here." My message didn't go through, and Ivy and I looked at each other at the same time. She must have tried as well.

"Apollo, what can we do for you?" Ivy kept her voice calm, but her stiff posture said she was nervous.

"A little birdy told me there were some nosy wolves trying to undermine my authority." He pushed off the front end and came around the passenger side. "What do you think you're going to do? Storm in there with no tactical training and save them all? People will die."

"What are you doing to save them?" Ivy's eyes flashed silver, and I gripped her hand a little harder just in case she lost her mind and attacked him.

"A good battle takes time to plan." Apollo put his hands on his hips. "Do we need to lock you five up?"

"This isn't some battle of yours. How do we know you're not working with the OQ?"

Apollo frowned and his own eyes flashed silver. "You think I would do that?"

"You tried to kill me!" I could tell Ivy was done with this man. Nothing he could do or say would earn him forgiveness.

"I thought we were past this." Apollo shook his head. "You will soon learn that things in our world don't work the same as in your world. Artemis beat me fair and square."

"In a thumb war. Who decides people's lives using their thumbs?" Ivy was starting to sound a bit hysterical, and I put my hand on the small of her back.

The whole situation was crazy. I was sure when this was all over and I had time to fully process it, I would either laugh my ass off or crawl into a ball and wonder what the hell had just happened.

"Are you mocking me?" Apollo narrowed his eyes. "You're to leave the premises immediately and whatever you're up to is to be stopped, or I will lock the five of you up."

"If it were your daughter in that place, would you be waiting as long as you are? You're a god. You don't need backup." Ivy had clearly pressed the button because the next thing I knew Apollo had her pinned to the side of the SUV.

I lunged forward to help, but Apollo hit me with a glare that made me freeze in place. What the fuck?

"You know nothing about me, my daughter, or my sister. I suggest that you learn your place before I have to teach you." It was the most serious I'd heard him sound, and Ivy flinched back away from him.

If he hurt her, I'd kill him myself.

"Now, get in your vehicle and leave."

He didn't have to tell us twice.

∼

After having lunch at a small diner down the road and still seeing no movement on the tracking device, we decided to head back to Arbor Falls. The main goal had been to figure out where they were keeping the wolves, not to make any moves against them. There wasn't much the five of us could do.

As for Apollo? We wanted to steer clear of the unstable god as much as possible. He was a loose cannon and liable to snap one of our necks if we pushed him.

"Is it all right if I ride back with Cole and Silas?" Xander asked as we left the restaurant. He acted like nothing had happened while we ate, even though none of us knew exactly where he had gone.

Ivy should have done that creepy thing where she looked through his vision to see what he was up to, but she had agreed not to do that unless it was a life-or-death situation. Still, I worried about him. I worried about all of them.

"You don't like us anymore?" Ivy jokingly asked, sticking out her bottom lip in a pout.

Xander hooked his arm around her neck and pulled her close, giving her a sloppy kiss on her cheek. "I love you, baby. But I want to talk about rebuilding a Ford Mustang, not Twilight."

"You guys are always picking on me." She shoved him away as we got to the vehicles. "One of these days I'm just going to put a sign in front of my vagina that says it's closed for business."

"Does that mean the back door is open for business then?" Silas squealed and ran away as Ivy chased him.

Honestly, he was just doing it to get on her nerves. I thought it was funny as hell.

"Are you all right with me riding with them?" Xander cupped my jaw and kissed me softly.

"Why would I mind?" If anything, I was happy that he was finally getting along with Silas. For a while there, I thought he was going to kill him.

Did it bother me they'd been intimate with each other? When I'd first heard about Xander kissing Silas at the Spring Carnival, I had been, but that was only because it surprised the shit out of me. As for Xander helping Ivy with giving Silas a blow job? I just wished I had been there to watch.

We took off on the two in a half-hour drive back home. It was a beautiful day out, and I briefly wondered where in the hell the coalition's headquarters were. It had to be within a three-hour radius of Arbor Falls, but there weren't many places that fit the appearance of what we saw there. Had we even been on Earth? Was that even a thing?

"What are you thinking about? It looks like it hurts."

"I was just wondering if the coalition's headquarters were even on Earth."

She laughed. "You think there's another plane of existence? Like we went through a portal?" She made a sound like I was crazy, but there was a hint of a real question in her voice.

"Well, where else could it be? Could it have a protective barrier around it? You need to ask your mom if you can protect our territory with a protective bubble and see what she says."

Part of my constant wondering that made me lose sleep at night was that there were so many possibilities now that we knew gods existed. We still didn't know the full extent of Ivy's or Silas's capabilities. With Silas, we might not ever know because he refused to learn to be one with the trees. Something about not accidentally wanting to start growing bark on his dick.

All four of us being mates with her also raised a lot of questions. If we could help her heal Cole, what else could we help her do?

"I think there's a lot that needs to be explained to us, but part of me doesn't want to know because I don't plan on being part of that world. I'm a wolf, not a goddess." Her voice held a finality that sent a shiver down my spine.

"What if the things you learn come in handy and help our kind?" I glanced over at her, and her brows were furrowed in thought. "That doesn't mean you have to go into stasis or give up your wolf. At least I don't think."

"I don't want to attract too much attention to myself. I already do with the color of my hair and the fact that I'm a female alpha. Let's not forget that I have four mates, and you're all hot."

"You think I'm hot?"

"Have you seen yourself? You're poster worthy. Tape to the ceiling above the bed hot."

I laughed and my chest puffed out. I knew I was an attractive guy, but hearing it from my girlfriend was that much sweeter.

"We should get posters made of me and hang them around the house when everyone else is asleep." I grinned. That would drive Cole nuts. "I can take a picture lounging on the bed with my stuffed squirrel covering my dick."

"Like he's protecting your nuts. I like it. That would be really sexy." Ivy's hand found its way over the center console and landed right on my crotch. "But I think the picture would be even better if you could see everything. You have a very nice dick."

"We still have an hour and a half until we get home." My dick twitched in my pants as she slowly slid her hand across my jeans.

Damn it, what was this woman doing? I needed to focus on driving, not how hard my dick was getting as she rubbed me.

"You could find somewhere to pull over." She trailed her fingers up and down my shaft as it slowly hardened.

There was no way I was going to be able to focus on safety with her hand on my crotch and my dick as hard as a rock. There was no way I'd stay on the road if she started giving me a hand job. I needed to find somewhere private to pull off.

"What about up here? It looks like there's nothing besides trees." She wrapped her hand around me as far as it would go with my jeans on and squeezed. "Unless you want me to take you out while you're driving."

I flipped on my blinker and pulled off the highway, deciding that the best direction to turn would be toward the orchards.

"Let me just text the guys and tell them we're making a pit stop." She took her hand off my dick, and I groaned.

About a minute off the highway, I turned down a dirt road that ran between two orchards. It didn't seem like anyone else was doing any work, so hopefully, no one would happen upon us.

As soon as I put the SUV in park, Ivy leaned across the console and pressed her lips against mine. Our tongues collided, and my dick wept in my pants. I reached down, popped the fly, and pulled down the zipper, my erection springing free.

"Look how hard you are for me." She licked her lips and then leaned across to wrap her lips around the head, sucking lightly.

I couldn't stop the urge to thrust up into her mouth. I was so damn horny just from her touching me through my jeans. With her mouth on me, it was all over.

She licked the underside of my cock, her eyes finding mine and lighting up with mischief. "You want to fuck my mouth?"

"Yes," I hissed, my hand grabbing onto her ponytail. "Tell me."

When we first started having sex, I wasn't much of a dirty talker, but it made her so damn wet that now I couldn't resist.

"I want you to open that pretty little mouth of yours so I can stick my cock inside it nice and slow. And then I'm going to fuck it."

She moaned against the underside of my crown and I nearly whimpered from how good it felt.

"Are you going to let me fuck your mouth, sweetheart?" I gave her ponytail a light tug, and she moved onto her knees. "Are you going to swallow me down that throat of yours and then drink my cum?"

"Fuck. Yes. I want to drink all of you."

"Then open your mouth."

She opened and wrapped her lips around me as she slowly took me in. I put my head back against the headrest. There was nothing like her mouth wrapped around me. Nothing.

With one hand on the back of her head and the other on the door handle, I began thrusting up into her mouth as she sucked around my hard length, getting deeper and deeper with each thrust. I could already feel my balls pulling close to my body, getting ready to explode inside her mouth.

"Just like that. Let me fuck your mouth. Take it all the way."

I hit the back of her throat, and she gagged slightly, only making me even more turned on. Her hands worked inside my pants and cupped my balls.

"Fuck, fuck, fuck. I'm going to explode." Gripping her hair, I pulled her off me and up to my mouth, our lips colliding in a feverish and sloppy kiss.

My hand went between her legs, finding her scorching through the thick material of her jeans. Our lips broke apart, both of us panting, our noses touching.

"Back seat?" She started to climb over the center console, but I stopped her. "Not so fast."

Looking around, I decided I just couldn't wait any longer and put her in her seat. "Take off your pants and recline your seat all the way back."

She quickly shimmied out of them as I pulled my own off. I climbed over the center console and situated myself between her legs. My fingers dipped into her folds, feeling how wet she was for me. I brought them to my lips and licked them clean as she watched with hooded eyes. I moved one of her legs and put it on the windowsill then bent her other leg at the knee.

I sank into her, my lips finding her neck and sucking on her sensitive flesh.

"You feel so good," she breathed as I began moving in and out of her. "Fuck, right there."

I began pounding into her, not wanting to waste any more time. I could feel the SUV rocking with each thrust and knew if anyone came by, they would know exactly what we were doing inside.

I didn't care.

My balls tightened, and I exploded inside her, her own release following not long after mine, squeezing every drop out of me. I collapsed on top of her, wishing we were at home so I didn't have to move.

"Fuck, Eli. That was intense."

It was, and we would definitely be doing it again soon.

CHAPTER THIRTEEN

Ivy

It had been two days since we placed the tracker and there hadn't been any movement on it. Eventually, they would go to the storage unit, but until then, we were impatiently waiting.

I'd done a conference call with all the alphas in California, Oregon, and Nevada to update them on the issue. Half said they would follow the coalition's lead, and the other half agreed that if the coalition wasn't going to act soon, we should.

I didn't think Artemis knew anything about the coalition knowing the wolves' whereabouts, and the last thing I wanted was for her to get hurt going after them on her own.

She was still staying in the guest room, and as

quirky as she was, I was starting to grow quite fond of her.

Well, until training went from mental to physical.

Someone had given the woman a coach's whistle, and every time she blew it, I was supposed to reach down inside of myself, grab my power, and run across the clearing at a blinding speed.

There wasn't a lot of speed, but there was a lot of panting. She was annoyingly patient with me. Each failed attempt she would zoom across to me and pat me on the back.

"You need more motivation. Wait at the starting point, and I'll be right back." She vanished, and I turned around in a circle, still not believing she could move that fast.

Grumbling, I jogged back to the starting line. It was already ninety degrees out and my workout clothes were drenched with sweat and water I'd dumped on myself. I was going to need to hose off outside before going into the house later.

It hadn't even been more than two minutes and she was back, dropping Silas onto the ground. She'd carried him all the way from the house that fast?

"You lunatic! Now that vase is going to be ruined and I've been working on it for two hours!" Silas jumped to his feet and dusted off his ass. "Fuck."

He brought his hands away, which were now covered in dirt and grass as well as clay.

"Where do you think the word lunatic comes from?" She cocked her head to the side, a grin on her face. "Now run."

Silas squealed as he began to run across the clearing, but not from his own free will.

"What the fuck?" My mouth was hanging open, and Artemis reached over and pushed up my chin.

"Go get him. He's headed straight for a rocky downward slope." She started humming to herself, walking in the direction Silas had just gone.

Was she fucking nuts?

"He won't die, but he'll break a lot of bones."

I sprinted after him as he entered the trees. I knew exactly what area he was headed for, and if he fell down it, he'd probably break his neck.

Reach inside for your strength.

I could feel it, but taking hold of it seemed impossible.

"Ivy! Do something! Fuck!" He was starting to freak out and flail his arms.

"I'm trying!" I was still too far behind him to stop him, even at my normal speed. His feet were moving alarmingly fast.

"I'm going to die! Oh my God, I'm going to die, and I never even got to stick it in your butt!" He let out a blood-curdling scream as the forest sloped downward and his feet began moving faster.

I wanted to laugh and cry all at the same time, but I needed to focus. I could just shift, and that would give me an extra little boost of speed, and I might be able to stop him in enough time. That wasn't the point of the exercise, but I also couldn't let him fall and tumble down a rocky slope.

I released a war cry and somehow, someway, the

power just came to me as I was reaching for it and the burst of speed sent me flying straight past him. Now I was going to be the one dying.

Before I made it far enough down the slope to get to the part that was steeper and rocky, I was suddenly frozen in place.

"Excellent." Artemis clapped her hands together and then I was on my ass, the wind knocked out of me.

"I'm never going to be the same after this." Silas was talking to himself, and I looked over my shoulder to find him flat on his back, staring up at the trees.

"You'll be fine. Now, let's go back the other way. I was thinking this time I'd have him run backward." Artemis giggled, and I was starting to wonder how in the hell she'd managed to give birth to me.

~

"BUNNY, you owe me so much sex for this," Silas complained as we both trudged back to the house.

The sun was already setting, and we had been at it for hours. Just when I thought I'd finally gotten the hang of it, Artemis said she had to go and then disappeared at the same spot where Apollo had the day he shot Cole. There had to be a magical portal or something there.

"I'm sorry about your vase." I grabbed his hand and threaded our fingers together. "I can help you make a new one."

"Are you saying that you want to recreate the scene from *Ghost*?" He looked over at me and smiled even though he looked exhausted. "That could be really hot. Both of us naked, sitting behind my pottery wheel, clay splattering all over our bodies."

I rolled my eyes and laughed. "I probably wouldn't be much help if I was naked. You'd be distracted."

"Everything is better naked. It might inspire my creative juices." He squeezed my hand. "Don't let Artemis push you too hard. Six hours is a long time to be running sprints. I'm surprised you didn't pass out."

"It was weird. Every time I started to feel weak or thirsty, she waved her hand in front of me and it went away." I could see how learning what I was capable of might one day come in handy, but it was overwhelming. There was a lot I could already do that I needed to practice. Learning more might make my head explode.

"What are you going to do with this newfound speed?"

"Tomorrow, if I can walk, I'll challenge Cole to a race." I swung our arms back and forth as we walked. I really was enjoying the stroll through the forest hand-in-hand with him. It wasn't often we got to do things like this. "What do you think the loser should have to do?"

He made a noise like he was thinking. "Wear a butt plug."

I laughed so hard my stomach hurt. His obsession with anal sex was borderline ridiculous, but it brought much laughter to the bedroom and to conversation, so I wasn't about to tell him to stop.

"You should be in the race too."

"Hell no. I won't tell him how fast you are, but there

ain't no way I'm racing you." He let go of my hand and wrapped an arm around my waist, moving me closer to him. "Besides, I don't need to lose a bet to wear a plug. All you have to do is ask, and I'll try it. Unlike someone I know."

"One of these days you're going to tease me when I'm in a bad mood." I grinned over at him and made a slicing gesture across my neck.

"I'm impatiently awaiting that day." Silas stopped right before we got to the yard and pulled me against the front of him, running a hand down my cheek and across my collarbone.

I shivered under his touch as he slowly leaned in and took my lips in the most gentle and sweetest kiss he'd ever given me. We stood there for a few minutes, kissing leisurely, and then he pulled away, took my hand, and led me back to the house.

If we had a pool, I could have just jumped in and felt ten thousand times better. I was determined to have one at the new house, even though there was a pond. We could have Riley and her men come stay with us either way, and that excited me.

We walked into the house, and the scent of pizza hit my nose. There was nothing like burning a gazillion calories and then stuffing one's face with cheesy, meaty goodness.

I couldn't see all the way into the living room from the angle we were at, but besides the sounds from the television, there was a buzzing noise and then Cole's husky laugh.

Oh my sweet fawn. Were they using a vibrator?

"I think I'm going to be sick." Silas grabbed my arm, pulling me to a stop. "Help me up the stairs. I need to shut my eyes."

"What are they-"

"Ow, fuck!" Xander hissed.

"Just breathe. I told you it was going to hurt until you adjusted to it." What the fuck was Manny doing with my men?

The second I could see them, I sighed in relief. "Tattoos? In the middle of the living room?"

They had set up a tattoo table where the coffee table used to be and had pizza and beers on another folding table. The television had some kind of fight on.

"I told Cole we should do it in the garage, but he said it was too hot." Eli came from down the hall, carrying his laptop. "We ordered pizza and wings."

"I'm going to go shower real quick." I moved closer to the tattoo table and Cole blocked me from seeing. "What are you doing?"

"You can't see yet! Go shower, come back and eat, then help me convince Silas to get one too." Cole gave me a quick peck and then herded me toward the stairs.

After showering, I hunted down Silas who was in his bedroom, lying on the bed with a towel still wrapped around his waist. I knocked on his open door and he turned his head.

"Are you that scared of needles?" I could hardly see his face with how dark he kept his room and moved in a few steps. "What's wrong?"

"Besides, what's happening downstairs?" He shut his eyes. "I'm tired as fuck, bunny."

I sat down on the edge of the bed. "I should have done something to stop Artemis."

"No, that needed to happen. It would have been nice if she'd asked instead of just flying right into my studio and snatching me away from my project." He sat up and ran his fingers through his damp hair. It was starting to get longer again, and I had to admit, I'd missed him with long hair. "I'm tired of not knowing if today is the day one of us dies."

"None of us are going to die." I reached over and squeezed his knee. "Look at all Cole has been through and he's still kicking."

I had the same fear as Silas, but if I freaked out about what the next few weeks or months might have in store for us, they'd all worry. For the time being, I was trying to ignore the danger that the OQ presented to all of us, not just the wolves they held captive.

Silas took my hand and flipped it over, tracing the lines on my palm. "I can't wait until we can just get on my motorcycle and go for a drive without having to worry if someone is following us or if we'll be attacked."

"I've only been on the back of a motorcycle once and it was because I was dared." I shivered as he brought my hand to his lips and kissed the palm before kissing my wrist. "Silas..."

My nipples immediately stood at attention as he trailed his lips across my skin. He looked up at me with innocent eyes and I damn near threw myself at him, but then my stomach let out the loudest rumble I'd ever heard.

"Hungry for my dick or pizza?" He chuckled and scooted off the bed. "I wonder what it would feel like to have you lick pizza sauce off my dick."

"That would be messy, but tasty." I stood and walked to the door. "Chocolate would be better."

He dropped his towel and grabbed a pair of clean boxers that were practically hanging out of his drawer. He at least contained most of his disorganization to his bedroom. Not that Cole would allow him to make a mess anywhere else.

"Can you bring me up a few slices of pizza and some wings?" Silas grabbed his iPad and flopped back onto the bed.

Laughing, I picked up his towel and hung it on the doorknob so the carpet wouldn't get damp. "You're seriously going to stay up here?"

"Yes. Call me a wuss if you want, but I know myself and being around needles..." He inhaled sharply.

"You can sit far away from it. Don't stay up here alone." I walked to his dresser and pulled out a pair of shorts. "Just pretend the buzzing is a vibrator."

I threw the shorts at his head and he grunted, putting his iPad down and getting back up. "If I faint or vomit..."

"You won't. If you feel sick, maybe I can touch your head and make your fear go away." I was joking, but part of me did wonder just how far my healing abilities went.

Silas followed me back downstairs, his anxiety nearly palpable as we grabbed food and sat on the end of the couch farthest from the tattooing. I couldn't tell what Xander was getting, but they said it was the size of my palm.

Cole apparently had already gotten his, but had his shirt on to cover it. With wolf healing, he didn't even have to have plastic wrap or whatever else they put on new tattoos.

"Eli, are you getting one?" I finished the last bite of my pizza and took a drink from my beer.

"It will be my first tattoo, but yes." He turned toward us. "It's not that I haven't wanted a tattoo, I just haven't wanted to take the time to get one."

"I'm never getting one." Silas took my empty plate with his and put them on the table. "I don't care if you three all have matching ones."

I looked between him and Eli. "This was planned?"

"We didn't know when Manny was going to have time." Eli flipped through the channels on the television since the fight they had been watching was over.

"And they match? You aren't tattooing my name, are you?"

"It would have been a lot faster to get your name." Xander laughed, and Manny let out a frustrated growl.

The special report music played from the television and the words *Breaking News* flashed across the screen.

"This is Brittany Aspen coming to you live from the state capital, where there are rabid wolves running loose. At this time, we are being told that local authorities have urged residents to stay indoors while the situation is handled. The capital and surrounding businesses are on lockdown until

they can safely leave. It's unclear at this hour how the wolves got to the middle of the city or where they came from. We will keep you updated as this story unfolds."

We were all silent as we stared at the television screen, watching a video clip of two wolves chasing a man in a suit across the lawn. The video cut off and showed a map with red dots to indicate where the wolves were.

"Jesus." Manny put his tattoo gun down. "I'm finished. Eli, I guess we'll have to wait to do yours."

Xander sat up abruptly, his eyes glued on the television. In the center of his chest, a tattoo of a red wolf stood out against the paleness of his skin.

I wanted to cry, both because they were getting tattoos of my wolf and because of what was unfolding on the television screen.

"I know that wolf." Xander stood and moved closer to the television. "That's Cal."

"Your pack mate?" Eli went and stood next to him, putting a hand on his back. "Are you sure?"

Xander nodded.

"Alpha?" Rory's voice was calm but had an edge to it.

"Yes?" I moved toward the kitchen where I could concentrate on her voice more. It was difficult to be around noise when someone was speaking in my head.

"We have a situation near the eastern clearing. There's a bloodied woman, but we can't understand a word she says."

"I'll be right there." I went back to the living room where the television was back to the show that was on. "There's a woman in our territory. I need to go assess the situation."

"I'll go with you." Silas and Cole both jumped out of their seats, speaking at the same time.

"This is too coincidental." Eli got to his feet. "We'll all go."

A month ago, I would have rolled my eyes, but now there was safety in numbers. It was also becoming clearer and clearer with each training session that I had access to more power if they were close by.

It was hard to believe that three months ago I had no clue I was anything other than human. I still sometimes wondered if I was going to wake up from a coma and have it all be a figment of my imagination.

As we undressed, I pushed away the thought that this might become an even bigger nightmare before the night was over.

CHAPTER FOURTEEN

Silas

We ran through the forest as a united front. I could feel everyone's nervousness as we neared the clearing where the bleeding woman was.

I couldn't wait for everything to be over so I could enjoy my new life a little more. It wasn't that it wasn't enjoyable already, but every five minutes something seemed to cause a setback.

From the moment I met Ivy, there had been nothing but roadblock after roadblock to our happiness. One day, I'd look back on everything and know it was what brought us together and made us strong. But right then, I really just wanted a refund.

Unfortunately, it was a nonrefundable ticket.

"I don't recognize the scent." Cole was running slightly

ahead of us all. I really wanted to yell at him for putting himself in harm's way again, but would save that for later. *"Doesn't smell human either."*

"What do you mean it's not human?" I sped up so we were running side by side and sniffed the air. *"It smells earthy. That's weird."*

A sense of familiarity filled me at the smell, and a whimper escaped. We were almost to the clearing and my stomach twisted the closer we got.

"Ivy, don't-" Cole's words meant nothing because she darted past us, using some of her newfound speed. *"What the fuck?"*

So much for the butt plug bet.

"It's Griselda!" Ivy's communication was laced with worry.

We pushed ourselves and entered the clearing, finding Griselda speaking a mile a minute. "They came out of nowhere! I didn't know what to do, so I called for Artemis, but I couldn't just let them kill all the hinds. Most of the agents were gone on an urgent mission, and it was just me and a few others. There was so much blood."

Ivy shifted and knelt next to her, taking her bloodied hands. "I don't understand what you're saying, Griselda."

"You must understand!" She let out a frustrated wail. "Artemis went back. You must go! She can't fight them alone!"

Ivy turned her head and looked at us. "What do you think she's saying?"

I shifted, confused as all fuck. "You can't understand her?"

"No. Can you?" When I nodded, Ivy's eyes widened and she turned her attention back to Griselda, who had a giant wound on her leg. "How can you... holy shit, is she a dryad?"

She let out another cry and grabbed at her leg. Ivy's hands glowed as she worked on healing her.

"I'm a nymph. Speaking in your tongue is too difficult right now." Griselda looked at me, panting. "Your mother was a good friend."

A pain stabbed through my heart, and I stumbled forward a few steps. Cole grabbed onto my arm, steadying me.

"Who attacked? Wolves?" As much as I wanted to talk about my mom, the whole reason we were there in the first place was more pressing.

"Yes. I don't know how they got through the protections." She hissed as her wound closed. "Please, hurry."

I repeated what she had said previously and knelt down to take her hand. "How do we get there?"

She pointed to where Apollo and I had fought. "There's a ley line. Only the gods can access it. Ivy should be able to follow it to our sanctuary."

"How did you get here?"

"Artemis. She told me to warn you that the war has begun." She squeezed my hand. "You must stop them before they destroy everything."

I stood, my resolve to take down the OQ and whoever was behind it burning in my gut. "There's a ley line that Ivy can follow to get us to where we need to go."

Jogging over to the spot where the symbol always appeared, I put my hands on my hips, not seeing it.

"I don't want to splice us or something." Ivy approached, and as she did, the symbol appeared out of nowhere. "Huh. All it took was me visualizing it."

"This isn't Harry Potter... at least, I don't think. Can we all go together?"

"She didn't say we couldn't." I grabbed Ivy's hand and then Cole's. "Let's go."

"Are you going to be okay or do you want to stay here?" Ivy grabbed Xander's hand. "It will be fine if you want to stay."

"We're stronger together." Xander grabbed Eli's hand, shut his eyes, and took a deep breath. "Let's do this."

Ivy looked over to the other wolves. "Get her to the house and call Trevor."

She started running, us right along with her, and then it was like we were in one of those vacuum tubes at the bank. At first, it felt like I had too much to drink and the world was spinning. Then a feeling of weightlessness overcame me before I felt like I was being pulled to a stop.

The trip lasted what felt like less than a minute and then my ears popped as we stopped right at the edge of the forest where the coalition's headquarters were.

"I think I'm going to be sick." Cole rushed to a bush and dry heaved.

"We should have thought this through a little more."

I looked down at my dick hanging limp against my thigh. "I'm assuming we're going to shift?"

"I am. I don't need my dick bitten off." Cole shuddered as he came back to join us. "What's the plan, Alpha?"

"I think before we make any decisions, we need to assess the situation and see how many wolves are here. Let's stay like this until we need to shift. It's harder to smell us when we're human."

We crept toward the tree line, careful to stay hidden behind bushes and trees. It was hard to see much of what was happening because the barn was in the way and it was dark, but one thing was for sure; the smell of blood was ripe in the air.

"Should we go through the barn?" Ivy twisted her lips to the side in consideration. *"There might be weapons we can use inside."*

"Woah! We can hear each other now?" Every time we'd tried before, there was a block in place.

"That's strange. Maybe it's because I've been training." Ivy shrugged. Now wasn't the time to think about the whys of things in this place.

"It's too quiet." Cole sniffed the air. *"There's a lot of blood in the air. Shifters and animals. Ivy, if this all goes to shit, you, Eli, and Xander need to go back."*

"We aren't separating." She gave him a firm look and then darted across the small patch of grass to a pen outside the barn.

Dashing after her, we ducked into a pig pen that was empty. The barn was eerily quiet, and a chill ran down my spine. We crept across to a storage room and Ivy started pulling tools off the wall.

"Just in case." She handed me a hay hook.

It was a bit like having Wolverine hands, and I gripped the handle. *"No heroics. Let's scope things out then wait for backup."*

The barn doors were open so we had to move toward them carefully. Someone had let the animals out and their fate became evident as we got closer to the door and could see outside.

Before we could stop her, Ivy jumped forward and shifted, taking off across the lawn toward the house. What the fuck was she doing?

"Ivy!" She'd blocked us.

"Son of a bitch!" Cole threw his pitchfork down and took off after her.

I looked over at Xander and Eli. "Are you staying?"

"Going." Xander leapt away from Eli, shifting before either of us could stop him. He'd shifted just fine when we'd gone to find Griselda, but this was different. More was at stake.

Following them, we ran across the yard that was spotted with blood and dead animals. Bile burned my throat as we passed a few agents, not even shifted. We shouldn't have come without backup. We were headed straight toward certain death.

Ivy had stopped on the side of the house behind some bushes running down the sidewalk in front of the windows. It was just enough space for our wolves to walk single file without being detected.

"Sorry. I had to concentrate." Ivy led the way as we slinked along. *"I caught scent of Artemis."*

"This is stupid." Cole had his nose practically in her ass. I bet if she tried to take off again, he'd grab her tail. I would if I wasn't at the tail end of our caravan. *"Artemis can take care of herself."*

Artemis might have been a goddess, but if a hundred wolves attacked her, would she be able to stop them? What if Hera really was behind OQ and not just some group of cultists?

We stopped at the edge of the house.

"There are wolves just standing there like soldiers. At least a hundred." There was only space for Ivy to see around the corner. *"There are several men dressed in tactical gear with military style weapons."*

"There's not much we can do right now. We should go back home and wait." I didn't want us to risk being caught.

"Hold on. Something's happening." Ivy lowered herself to the ground and crept forward on her belly so we could all hide in the shrubs at the front of the house.

I could barely see through the leaves, but what I could see made my hair bristle.

Johnny, the agent who had vanished after the rescue mission to save our pack's wolves, stepped out of an SUV. He looked the same as before, but now he exuded power as he walked in front of the wolves.

"Where's Artemis?"

"She tried to stop us, but the net worked like a charm. You were right about her coming to stop us. She's secure." The man puffed out his chest. "Our distraction in Sacramento is working well. The agents that were still watching the warehouse were taken care of and the rest of our wolves are headed this way now."

"Good. What about the wolves from the Arbor pack?"

"Sir, they aren't fully trained." The man flinched as Johnny turned to stare at him. "They would be unpredictable in battle. We have another four hundred in the prison that are willing to fight for us, but they aren't trained like these ones are."

Johnny pinched the bridge of his nose. "We need those wolves. The others will keep them in line. If not, we'll kill them." He snapped his fingers. "And the redhead? Did we determine her origin?"

"Artemis has been staying with them. We aren't one hundred percent certain why."

"I think I know why; I just need to confirm it before I summon them. This is perfect. I never imagined all of this would fall into my lap." He rubbed his hands together. "Let's move out. We're done here. Get the prisoners ready to transport, and I'll make some calls."

We waited until they started loading the wolves into vehicles before crawling back the way we came.

"We need to contact your dad so we can get into contact with Apollo." Ivy looked back at me. *"As much as I don't want him involved, he isn't going to be happy they have Artemis."*

"Who do you think they were talking about summoning? Hera?" Eli was right in front of me and was trembling slightly. I wanted to nuzzle him, but we weren't exactly in a good position for that.

"Who else would they summon?" Cole grunted. *"Let's get back to Arbor Falls. We need to make sure all the wolves that were captured by OQ are locked down."*

That meant me, Eli, and Xander too.

Fuck.

~

THE TRIP back along the ley line wasn't nearly as bad as the first time using it. It was like Ivy had her own high-speed rail system at her disposal. Maybe there was a whole network of them and we could go anywhere we wanted.

All the possibilities distracted me briefly, and I didn't even notice that everyone had come to a screeching halt, staring at a tree in the middle of the clearing.

I rubbed my eyes. "What the hell?"

The newest beta trainees, Rory and Owen, got up from where they were laying under the tree and shifted back to their human forms.

Ivy stared up at the tree and her eyes widened. "Is this..."

"She rattled off some more stuff in that language and then the next thing we knew a tree was growing from the ground and she walked right into it and disappeared into the trunk." Rory shook her head in disbelief. "I had to wonder if someone had slipped me a hallucinogen."

With my mouth hanging half open, I approached

the tree and put my hand on the trunk. "Griselda, are you all right?"

The leaves rustled and I dropped my hand and backed up. I was a little freaked out about this revelation. Did that mean I could turn into a motherfucking tree?

"Hey. Don't freak out about this. Artemis said to preserve yourself you'd join with a tree. That's probably what she's doing to heal herself." Ivy had stepped up beside me and took my hand. "We need to get back to the house."

"Oh! Sara wanted you to contact her when you returned," Owen said. "She said it was urgent."

Ivy let go of my hand and looked over at the trees. I could tell by the look on her face that she was connecting with Sara to find out what was wrong. With enough practice, she wouldn't contort her face anymore in concentration.

"The tracker in the dog food is on the move north. She's watching it closely. With everything that's happened, we can't trust that the tracker hasn't been compromised." Ivy let go of my hand and shifted, taking off toward the house.

The moon was high in the sky and I stared up at it for a minute before following. I'd have to enjoy the moon another night.

CHAPTER FIFTEEN

Ivy

Artemis had just come into my life and now all of that was at risk. I didn't understand how a net could stop a goddess, but it had to be something special to be able to capture her.

The question was, why did Johnny want her so badly and what did it have to do with Hera.

It was nearly two in the morning by the time we got back to the house. I was exhausted, and I could see the weariness in my men too. We needed sleep, but also needed to prepare for what Johnny and OQ had in store for us.

Our clothes were right where we left them as we shifted on the deck. I grabbed mine with shaking hands and turned so they couldn't see how out of sorts I was.

"We need to alert all wolves that were taken by the

OQ that they are to lockdown or get far away from here." Cole was already half dressed by the time I even managed to pull on my pants. "Some have basements, but a lot don't."

"And what about us?" Eli threw his shirt over his shoulder, opting not to put it on. "I think we would be able to tell if we were brainwashed."

"Not necessarily." Locking any of them up wasn't something I wanted to do. "It's better we take every precaution necessary."

Silas wrapped his arms around me. "We want to protect you."

"You can't protect her if you're trying to rip out her throat." Cole opened the sliding glass door and I followed him in. "I hate it just as much as you do."

"Xander, are you coming?" Eli stopped just before following us inside. "What are you doing?"

The sound of helicopter blades made my stomach drop.

"Get inside, now!" Cole grabbed my arm and yanked me away from the door. I wanted to ask him what the hell he was doing, but then I heard it.

A shrill whistle.

Silas was halfway through the door when a growl ripped from him and he shifted, shredding his clothes. Eli and Xander were already lifting their heads to howl.

Cole kicked out with his foot, shoving Silas out the door. Silas bit into his leg and then yelped as Cole punched him and then slammed the door shut.

My heart was pounding so hard I could hardly hear what Cole was yelling at me.

Pushing past me, he flipped the table and moved it against the door, the glass cracking as three wolves ran into it. *My* three wolves.

"They'll hurt themselves!" I tried to connect to them, but there was nothing but chaos inside my connection with pleas of help from other pack mates.

I shut it down and backed away from the door. "Cole."

"Don't freak out." Cole rushed past me and came back less than a minute later with a gun.

I'd been frozen in place, shock setting in that this was it. This was the day I was going to have everything taken from me.

"I'm going to try to tranquilize them." Cole moved the table out of the way.

They weren't at the door anymore, but one or more of them was bleeding because a trail of blood went across the deck. I grabbed Cole's arm. "You're going to get hurt."

"I have to try." He opened the door and stepped outside. The helicopter was still somewhere nearby with the whistle sounding from its speakers. "I would tell you to stay inside, but I know you won't."

He was right.

I followed him onto the deck as we both scanned the yard. There were no wolves to be seen, but we could hear them in the forest. It sounded like they were moving toward the helicopter.

"Fuck." Cole put the gun in the waistband of his

pants. "We need to send out an alert and contact Trevor."

Once we were inside, I shut my eyes and opened my pack connection. It was like being hit with a million messages at once, and I stumbled back and covered my ears, my body trying to retreat from all the noise in my head.

Cole's arms enveloped me, and he nuzzled my neck. "Breathe. Block it all out."

I nodded and focused on making the connection one way. We hadn't had much time to practice it, so it took me longer than it should have to make the voices in my head go silent. I knew they were all freaking out.

"This is an urgent alert to all pack members. Shelter in place until further notice. Do not open your door for any wolves. If your loved one was previously taken by the OQ and they are still responsive, secure them in a locked room or basement, but be prepared to tranquilize them. All betas, beta trainees, and protection members are to report to the main house den immediately. Use caution and stay out of the forest to the North."

Silas's phone rang in the other room and Cole ran to grab it. "It's Trevor."

I growled. If he would have just moved in on the OQ, maybe we wouldn't be in the situation we were in now. Instead of dealing with a warehouse of wolves, we were dealing with them out in the open. We didn't even have the added benefit of my mom to help.

Fuck.

I grabbed my phone to find ten missed calls from Sara. I hadn't been sure if she would have shifted with the others. From what little she said of her time with the OQ, the younger women were kept separate from the men.

"Sara?" While I talked, I headed to the basement passage to get to the den.

"Where's my brother?" She sounded like she had been crying, and my own tears burned the back of my eyes.

"He shifted." I headed through the tunnel and up the stairs to the den. My voice was surprisingly calm given the situation. "We weren't able to tranquilize them in time."

I'd had my minor freak out back in the kitchen when it first happened, but now I had to put on my brave face for my pack. Not only were they depending on me to lead, but the entire mess was because of my fucked-up lineage.

"What are we going to do?" She sounded so lost, and I wanted to reach through the phone and hug her.

But it turned out, I could do it in person because she was already in the den's conference room along with Manny, her father, and Cole's parents. They all looked exhausted.

She had her laptop projected on the bigger screen showing a flashing blue dot of what I could only assume was the tracker. It was on the main highway headed straight toward Arbor Falls, but why would they be coming here?

"We need to intercept the truck. I don't like that they're headed this way."

"Is it possible they were keeping the wolves closer

than you thought?" Martha was sitting quietly in the corner, her eyes red rimmed. From lack of sleep or sadness, I couldn't be sure.

"Trevor just told me they were keeping the wolves in a warehouse off the interstate near the city. So, that's not it." Cole came into the room and immediately went to his mother for a hug. "They're going to intercept the truck."

I shut the door before any of the pack heard what we were talking about. We had been selective in sharing who the strangers hanging around were.

"The guy Johnny was talking to said something about capturing Artemis with a net. There's more at play here than just some cult." I watched out the window of the conference room as pack members began trickling in. "He said they needed all the wolves."

Juan was rubbing his daughter's back and stopped. "You said this Order of the Queen is something involving Hera? If a net was used to trap Artemis, it could be Hephaestus who is behind this." He laughed. "This doesn't seem real."

"It is real. Who the hell is Hephaestus?" I knew the basics of Greek mythology, and even then it seemed there were some inaccuracies.

"He's Hera's son. God of fire and metalwork. Born out of spite towards Zeus's infidelities and cast aside. Later was married to Aphrodite who cheated on him and he made a golden net to catch her in the act." Juan rattled off what he knew, and it was so outlandish that I wanted to laugh.

"What's your plan?" Walter was sitting with his arms

crossed and hadn't taken his eyes off me since I walked into the room.

Cole said his dad was actually pretty laid back when not having to deal with pack business, but so far all I'd seen was a gruff man who didn't accept me as an alpha. I could see how he'd be mad that a female took his son's place at the head of the pack, but he hadn't even given me a chance.

"I think we have a small window of opportunity to rescue our pack mates before chaos descends on us. If Johnny is a god, he doesn't seem to be able to use a ley line, or if he does, he might not know the one leading here from the coalition's headquarters exists." I paced in front of them. "We need to tranquilize our wolves. Do we have enough guns?"

"We have twenty. Each can be loaded with one dart at a time but have space for three additional darts to be loaded." Manny pulled a set of keys out of his pocket. "We'll need transport vehicles once they are down."

"The men will have guns." I sighed. "Should we tranquilize them first?"

"We should kill them first." Martha stood. "Do you have long range weapons?"

"A few that we just purchased." Cole put his hand on his mom's arm to stop her. "You aren't going."

Martha wheeled around and glared at him. "I am. I have excellent aim."

"I can use my bow and arrow." I moved out of the way so Manny could get out of the room. "Let's do this."

THE SKY WAS BARELY STARTING to lighten as we headed into the forest on foot. As soon as we were ready, we'd call in the off roading vehicles to help get our wolves back to safety.

Cole was quiet as we jogged along next to each other. We weren't trained for this type of fight, and it showed in the looks on everyone's faces. But we had to try.

It was eerily silent in the forest as we got closer to the scent of twenty of our pack mates. The females hadn't shifted, and a few of the males had been lucky enough to not be within range of the whistle.

We slowed down, keeping behind tree trunks as much as possible. My hands had begun to shake, and I grabbed my bow and nocked an arrow to keep myself from freaking out. A hand touched my elbow, and I looked over my shoulder to find Cole's mom.

"It will be okay," she mouthed.

I nodded, needing to believe she was right.

The wolves finally came into view and Cole held up his hand to stop our forward trajectory. The wolves were lined up in rows in a clearing similar to the one I frequented. I couldn't see Xander, Eli, or Silas, but I could sense them. I tried reaching out to them again, but it was like trying to wade through quicksand.

The helicopter had landed, and from what I could see, four men were there with guns ready on their shoulders. It was less than expected.

"I'll take the one on the left, and then Martha, Cole, and

Manny in that order. The rest of you fan out and tranq the wolf closest to you as soon as we fire."

Once everyone was in place, I counted down from three and we fired. The sounds of our weapons and the wolves yelping as they were hit filled the early morning sky.

No other men came out of the woodwork, so I called in the off roading vehicles that were waiting back at the den. I moved forward, Cole right beside me as wolves passed out. A few had already shifted back to their human forms.

"Where are they?" I turned in a circle and then rushed into the middle of the wolves. "They aren't here!"

Where the hell were my mates?

CHAPTER SIXTEEN

Xander

My head throbbed as awareness slowly returned. I'd fought the pull at first, but when Eli and Silas had shifted, my wolf had refused to ignore it any longer. I didn't remember much besides following them, joining together with a larger group, and then darkness.

I rolled over, the cold cement underneath me causing my chest to tighten. I was naked as the day I was born. Déjà vu overwhelmed me as I inhaled the scent of the basement.

How had we gotten to the basement?

"Ah, sixty-four. You always were the most stubborn of our wolves." The voice of my captor made my throat close up, and I gasped for air. "Your father was too soft when it came to you."

A piercing pain hit my side and I cried out, retreating to the far side of the cell. I never knew the man's name, but he was one of the worst, and he was here, standing with a shock stick in his hand.

"Did that hurt the poor, precious Alexander?" He tipped his head back and laughed. "Guess what? Daddy dearest isn't here to stop us from destroying you now."

Out of the corner of my eye, I saw two blurry lumps on the floor of the other two cells. I rubbed my eyes, trying to see what was going on better.

We were at our house, that was for certain, but I didn't understand why we were there with OQ and not with Ivy and Cole. Had they hurt them?

I reached out to Ivy and Cole, but I couldn't connect.

"Here. Put on some shorts. I don't want to stare at your dick any longer than I have to." He threw a pair into the cell and I reached for them with my foot, not trusting him not to shock me again. "Not even a thank you? I'll remember that." He went and sat in the small room that had monitors, his back to me.

I quickly slipped on the shorts and went to the bars to check on Silas and Eli. They were both passed out in their wolf forms still from whatever they had done to us.

The man wasn't paying me any attention now that he'd taunted me, so I tried the door with no luck. He was glued to the monitors, which showed different vantage points around the house and a few key spots of the territory. It was sunrise, the sky a light gray, and the colors coming to life with the rising sun.

"Water." My voice was hoarse, and I swallowed hard, trying to get moisture to it.

"Oh, for fuck's sake." The man got up, sending the chair crashing into the wall in the small room. "I should just let you die of thirst, but Johnny would crucify me for that."

He grabbed a bottle of water from the medical room and came back, handing it through the bars. I reached for it but then let it slip through my fingers. I let a whimper escape and looked down.

"You're a lame excuse for a man, aren't you?" He grunted as he bent down to pick it up, and that was when I made my move.

I lunged forward, grabbed his head, and slammed it into the bars. There was a crack, and he started to move away, but as soon as he turned I wrapped my arm around his neck, pulling him back to the bars.

My vision blurred as I grabbed onto my opposite hand and pulled back as hard as I could. He clawed at my arm, the sting of his nails doing nothing to dissuade me from choking him.

I was about to kill a man with my bare hands.

He went limp, but I didn't let up, counting until at least three minutes had passed. That seemed like a decent enough amount of time that if he was still alive, he would be hurt enough to be incapacitated.

I followed him down to the ground as he slumped against the bars and pulled his torso toward me. He had so many pockets and I hoped the keys to the cell doors were somewhere on him. We'd need to reevaluate leaving the keys hanging just inside the door leading down.

But why should we? Fighting for our lives nearly every day wasn't normal.

Or was it?

Was this our new normal?

The thought made me whimper as I dug in his pockets, pulling out everything from a gum wrapper with used gum, to a tranquilizer injector, to a cell phone. I rolled him over and sighed in relief as my fingers brushed a set of keys in his pocket.

With shaky hands, I unlocked the cell door on autopilot. How I was even able to function was astonishing.

Ivy.

Eli.

Silas.

Cole.

They were the reasons I was still trying. I nudged the guy with my foot, and he was unresponsive. He didn't appear to be breathing and I shut my eyes for a moment.

Another person dead at my hands.

Pushing my morbid thoughts about being a murderer aside, I went to the cell Eli was in and unlocked it. He was lightly snoring, his paws twitching slightly as if he was dreaming about running.

Most shifters didn't often sleep shifted, but when we did our wolves had vivid dreams of hunting and frolicking in the forest. Even during all the time I was locked up and then on the run, most of my dreams still had the freedom of the dirt beneath my paws.

I ran my hand over his stomach, marveling at how soft he was. I'd never actually petted Eli before. Most of the time he was in his human form, and when he was a wolf, we both were.

He whimpered and then his eyes popped open, making me curse in surprise. His lip curled back in a snarl and I backed toward the door.

"Eli?"

Before I could make it out of the cell, he was on top of me, knocking me onto my ass. His hot breath fanned across my face, and his teeth were so close to my nose that if I dared to breathe, I'd have touched them.

My wolf thrashed to break free and put him in his place, but I pushed back so hard it physically hurt to resist.

"Eli." The raspy voice drew his attention away from me for a second.

I brought my knees up and shoved him off, sending him flying into the bars and giving me a chance to scramble backward like a crab and pull the door shut.

His jaws snapped at the bars, and he swiped out with his claws, trying to maim me. My heart sank and I backed up. I couldn't lose him, not like this.

"Let me out." In the middle of Eli attacking me, Silas had shifted and seemed normal, but I couldn't be certain.

"Uh, maybe I shouldn't." My eyes were still glued on Eli, who hadn't given up trying to get to me.

"We need to get out of here and find out what's going on." He looked at Eli. "We'll have to leave him."

I knew he was right, but I didn't want him to be. I handed over the keys and stared down at Eli, who had finally stopped attacking the bars and had laid down. He was still snarling, but at least he wasn't going to hurt himself.

"I don't remember much of what happened besides the helicopter and the whistle." I rubbed the back of my neck. "I think you bit Cole."

"I did." He opened the door and put his hand on my shoulder. "He's safest here. I know he never talks about it, but what happened at that place really fucked him up."

"It fucked us all up." I turned and headed toward the surveillance room. "Holy shit."

On the back lawn was a small group of our pack—including Sara—surrounded by wolves that were sitting on their haunches like soldiers guarding prisoners. There were at least a hundred wolves.

"What the hell is their motivation?" Silas picked up an automatic rifle that had been left leaning against the wall. "I don't see Ivy or Cole anywhere."

"You don't think they..." I couldn't say it. I *wouldn't* say it.

"No." His eyes were scanning the camera feeds. "My dad is down the road. Let's go."

I followed him, not wanting to leave Eli behind but also not wanting to stay. We had been separated from the others for a reason and I just hoped that whatever their plan was, it didn't involve Eli.

"Let's leave him the key in case he shifts back." I went to the cell and put it just within reach. He watched me with a tilted head and growled. "I love you, Eli."

"We need to go, now." Silas had found some pants and was pulling them on. "We'll go out through the garage; I don't see any wolves or men around. That way we can grab some earplugs. I think I saw a container of them a few weeks ago on the workbench."

Once at the top of the stairs, Silas opened the door a crack and listened before moving into the hall. The garage was open, the off-road vehicles missing, but no one was inside. The earplugs were right on the workbench and Silas handed me a pair.

"You need a weapon."

After putting in my earplugs, I scanned the tools hanging over the workbench. What I needed was a gun, but as far as I knew, they were all locked in the den.

Silas said something to me, but his voice was muffled. I pointed to my ear, and he pushed me out of the way and grabbed a hammer before handing it to me. A hammer versus a gun wasn't going to get me very far, but if a wolf came at me, I'd be able to defend myself.

We darted across the road and into the cover of the trees. I tried to push Eli from my mind, but it was nearly impossible. We could have tranquilized him and carried him.

It wasn't long before we reached Trevor and the other coalition agents, parked down a driveway to another house. If five SUVs of agents was all they had, we were screwed.

"Dad." Silas took one of his earplugs out as we approached, and I did the same. "Please tell me there are more agents on their way."

Trevor cringed. "We had to leave half our agents in Sacramento to round up the wolves and another team is securing the truck with the dog food. We think they are going to attempt to take over our headquarters and use it."

"They used a helicopter and blasted a whistle to get our wolves. We woke up in our basement with one of the OQ's men watching us. We had to leave Eli behind." Silas moved to stand next to his father. "They have more wolves here now too."

"We know. We're strategizing with Cole and Ivy on how to best approach matters." Trevor held up a tablet that displayed the same video footage as in the surveillance room. "There are about twenty, including Ivy and Cole, that have been surrounded to the north. They did manage to tranquilize all of your pack mates affected by the OQ, but if we don't act soon, it will wear off."

"Where's Apollo?" I looked around for the god who had been nothing but a thorn in our side but might now be our only hope.

"Our agents that were around the warehouse the wolves were being kept, were compromised. Securing those wolves is of utmost importance since they are in a densely populated area." Trevor sighed. "We didn't tell him Artemis was captured because the success of the rescue was dependent on him helping. Wren, his daughter, will tell him once the job is done."

I whistled because that was going to be a tough piece of news to deliver. Apollo was a complete lunatic, but everything he'd done had shown how devoted he was to protecting his sister. Finding out she was captured? He'd lose his shit.

"Then what are we waiting for?" I wasn't about to let my mate die. "Let's go end this."

Even if that meant I might die myself.

CHAPTER SEVENTEEN

Ivy

It had been a trap and now we were surrounded by wolves. Cole already had his eye on the helicopter, and I knew exactly what he was thinking, but it wouldn't fit all of us.

The wolves weren't attacking us, but they were circled around the clearing, shoulder to shoulder, three rows deep. There were at least two hundred of them, if not more.

"Will the helicopter hold if we used it to protect ourselves?" There weren't many options available to us and now we just needed to wait on Trevor and the coalition.

"You saw what happened that one time the helicopter got attacked. They'd break through in no time."

Cole checked his phone. "They're heading this way. I'm not sure what their plan is, but if it goes to shit, you get in the helicopter with my mom and get out of here."

"Who's going to fly it?" I put my hands on my hips because there was no way I was leaving him or anyone else behind.

"Me." Martha came to stand next to me. She'd been quiet since we'd killed the four men. I couldn't tell if she still hated me or not. "I agree with my son that if things go awry, as many of us as possible need to get out of here."

"I'm not leaving my pack." I knew it was her pack too, but she hadn't been around for the last several months. "I'll die before letting any of these wolves hurt my family."

Martha's face softened and she sighed. "You'll be of no use to the pack if you're dead."

"I'll be of no use to the pack if I abandon those most vulnerable." I walked away from the helicopter. "I'm fighting, and if that means I go down with the ship, then that's the way it was meant to be."

My voice was surprisingly strong for being scared out of my mind, but then again, leaders could be scared and vulnerable, they just had to show they were willing to push past that to do what was right.

"I was wrong about you," Martha said softly before climbing into the driver's seat of the helicopter to prepare just in case.

I let out a shaky breath and then shook it off. Everything was going to be fine.

"Cover your mouths and noses! They're deploying sleeping gas!" Cole shouted just as what sounded like fireworks being shot out of their shells went off.

Cole grabbed me, pulling me against his chest as canisters landed all around us, smoke filling the air. It made me dizzy despite breathing through my shirt I'd put over my mouth and nose. We stood like that for at least two minutes, waiting for the smoke to clear.

"All clear!" Trevor shouted. "Let's move out!"

Seeing hundreds of wolves passed out looking like they were dead made emotion bubble up inside of me. Cole kept his arm wrapped around me as we stepped over the sleeping animals. A few of our team had breathed in the sleeping gas and were being carried, but we'd mostly gone unscathed.

Spotting Silas and Xander, I slipped from Cole's arms and ran to them, nearly knocking them down.

"Bunny." Silas buried his face in my neck, his arm tightly wrapping around my waist.

"Where's Eli?" Cole caught up to us as we headed back toward the house.

"We had to leave him locked up. He wouldn't shift back." Xander sounded almost detached, and I studied him carefully.

He looked dead on his feet, and I took his hand. We all looked a little worse for wear, not getting any sleep the night before. Now that backup had shown up, hopefully, everything would be over soon.

"We had a similar situation outside your house with wolves surrounding a group. My other team should be reporting any minute on their progress." Trevor was all business as we walked through the forest. "No reports on the whereabouts of Artemis or Johnny."

"He has to be somewhere close. How else did so many wolves get here, unless they have just been carting around trucks full of wolves to deploy." Cole's father was walking side by side with Trevor.

"If one good thing comes from this, maybe our dads don't try to kill each other every time they're in the same room." Cole sounded hopeful as he came up beside Silas and put his hand on his shoulder. "Are you okay?"

"I should be asking you that." Silas looked down at Cole's leg. "Sorry for biting you."

"It healed quickly. I barely even noticed it, honestly. But from now on, the only time I want you biting me is in the bedroom." Cole chuckled and then abruptly stopped when both Trevor and Walter looked over their shoulders with wide eyes.

"Can we focus on saving the pack instead of bedroom talk?" Walter turned back around, shaking his head.

I laughed and then took a deep breath. We could do this. We could save our pack mates and the other wolves that were being used as weapons.

As soon as the wolves came into view, Trevor raised his hand to stop us. With some elaborate hand movements that made no sense to me, his men spread out. It sounded like he was talking to himself, but then I saw the small earpiece in his ear.

"The wolves were too spread out for the others to

get them all in one go. We're going to deploy sleeping gas again. It might knock out the hostages, but that's better than the alternative."

After the canisters were shot into the areas surrounding the house, we moved closer. I tried reaching out to Eli again, but it was useless.

Just as we moved out from the trees, a whistle blew and howls came from all directions. Xander's hand squeezed mine so tightly it felt like he was going to break bones. He didn't shift though, the earplugs he had in stopping the whistle from having too much of an effect on him.

Silas wasn't so lucky.

He'd had an earplug in one of his ears, but the other had been out so he could talk to us. He shifted before any of us could try to bring him out of his trance.

Gunfire erupted a second later, sending us for cover anywhere we could find it. Some agents went back into the forest, some ran for cover behind the buildings on the property.

Cole grabbed for Silas, uncaring he was snapping and growling. He managed to grab him in a bear hold, but with bullets flying and Silas going nuts, it was short-lived.

Johnny came out of the house, a wolf being dragged by two men behind him. The wolf was struggling to free itself, its jaws snapping and growls feral sounding.

Eli.

Silas took off right for them.

"Silas! No!" Cole grabbed me around the waist,

yanking me back behind a tree. "Let me go! He's going to get shot!"

A pained yelp came from Silas, and he skidded across the ground on his stomach from his momentum. Johnny held up his hands and the gunfire stopped.

"Bunny..." Silas's pained voice pushed through whatever block there had been. *"Love you..."*

I elbowed Cole and his grip loosened on me, giving me just enough freedom to get away from him. He ran after me with a curse as I sprinted for Silas.

Did I care that Johnny might have his men open fire again? No.

I dropped to my knees next to Silas. He had at least five bullets that had hit him. It was like they had purposely shot at him.

Cole made a strangled noise as he dropped to the ground next to me. "This is bad."

Swallowing the bile that had worked its way into my throat, we dug the bullets out with our fingers. He was already passed out, and I couldn't tell if he'd stopped breathing.

"I'm going to heal him."

"But everyone will see." Cole grabbed my wrist to stop me from putting my hand over one of the wounds.

"I don't care." I could hardly see as Cole let go of my hand, and I placed it over the first bullet hole.

Everything was silent around us, like everyone was watching and waiting to see what I'd do. But then again, no one was coming after us because the odds of us being shot were highly likely.

My hands glowed faintly as I began healing Silas.

Cole put his hand over mine, his touch reminding me that I could utilize him to help heal.

I could sense Xander nearby and reached for his energy. He might not have been able to be out in the middle of the chaos with us, but just him being nearby made me stronger.

The last wound was closing up when a deranged laugh came from the direction of the house.

Johnny stopped at the edge of the deck, his eyes on me. "I knew it!" A grin spread across his face as he jogged down the stairs and stopped, pulling out a golden knife. "You are her daughter!"

He sliced open the palms of his hands and held them to the sky. "Zeus! Hera! I summon thee!"

Lightning cracked across the sky and the ground jolted, knocking us on our asses. A bright light flashed, and I shielded my eyes as I scrambled back up to my knees.

Silas whimpered, his head lifting off the ground a fraction of an inch before he let out a heavy sigh and let it fall back to the ground.

"Hephaestus." The booming voice was so powerful that the few loose strands of my hair blew in my face.

This was no ordinary man.

I unshielded my eyes and the man looked straight at me before looking at Johnny.

Zeus.

He looked nothing like what I had imagined. Instead of having gray hair and a beard, he had short brown hair and was clean shaven. He was insanely muscular with biceps I probably couldn't even wrap two hands around.

But it was the staff in his hand that confirmed that he was, in fact, the god of all gods. It was crackling with lightning, ready to strike down anyone and anything that came for him.

He looked around, his molten silver eyes taking in all the passed out wolves. "What is this?" The ground shook as he bellowed.

Suddenly, Johnny flashed across the yard and grabbed me by the hair. I'd been so distracted by Zeus, I hadn't even been keeping an eye on him, none of us had. He practically dragged me to where Zeus had landed. He shoved me to the ground at the god's feet.

"This is evidence that Artemis has broken her vow!"

I looked up at the man—the god—in front of me. This was my grandfather, and the thought made a giggle burst from me. I was losing it. It had taken several months, but my psyche was finally done for.

"Child, why are you laughing? Do you find this funny?" His voice was so loud I covered my ears. "Where is Artemis?"

"Bring her!" Johnny shouted.

Around the side of the house, three men were leading Artemis with guns pointed right at her head. Why wasn't she fighting them?

Our eyes met, and she gave me a tight smile and a slight shake of her head. That was when I saw it. What looked like a necklace was actually a golden net wrapped around her neck. Her hands were behind her, and I couldn't see them, but they probably were secured.

The men shoved her to the ground next to me and I caught her before she could face-plant into the grass.

"Father." She looked up at him with an impassive expression on her face. "Do not hurt my daughter for my transgressions."

Zeus's staff shot a bolt of lightning into the sky. I didn't quite know if I was frightened or in awe.

"Stand, child."

"Run. We'll distract them." Cole's command somehow made it to me, but it was pointless. There was no outrunning this.

Not knowing if he meant me or Artemis, I stood right along with my mother. I took a deep breath, hoping to suck up some courage to stand before someone that could probably turn me to ash by pointing his staff at me.

"How old are you, dear?" His question shocked me, and I looked up at him with wide eyes. They were the bluest of blues, and I found myself mesmerized by them. "Did I ask it wrong?"

"No, sweetie. She's in shock." A woman came from seemingly nowhere and stood next to Zeus before walking forward and cupping my cheek. "She's of strong lineage."

"Get your hands off my daughter," Artemis growled.

The woman, who I could only guess was Hera, rolled her eyes and backed up a step. "I see your immaturity is still intact."

Finally finding my voice, I hoped it didn't waver. "I'm twenty-six."

His eyes landed on Artemis. "For twenty-six years you kept my granddaughter from me?"

Lightning cracked across the sky, and I flinched as it hit the greenhouse, shattering some of the glass. He wouldn't hurt his own flesh and blood, would he?

Okay. Maybe he would.

"Do what you must to punish me, but leave her out of it. She is an innocent child, the product of a man and a woman who loved each other." Artemis stood taller. "Send me to the stars. Take away my abilities. Anything but harming her or those she loves."

"Very well." He shrugged, and I held my breath, waiting for the lightning to crash down on my mother.

He tipped his staff toward her, and I screamed as a bolt shot from it. It wrapped around her, sizzling as it went. It was over in a second and then Artemis was rubbing at her neck with her freed hands.

"You aren't angry with me?" Artemis sounded very confused and reached over to take my hand. I felt comfort in her touch, and I wondered if she was using some kind of special ability to calm my racing heart down.

"Why would I be angry? You were a child when you swore your chastity to me. I didn't think I had to tell you it was ridiculous once you were old enough."

"What? She went back on a sworn oath! Does fealty mean nothing!" Johnny had been standing off to the side next to his mother. "If word gets out that the all-mighty Zeus has allowed an oath be broken-"

"Enough." Zeus pinned him with a glare that would have made me piss my pants if it had been aimed at me. "What is this blasphemy you've caused here?"

Zeus turned to look at all the wolves, and in that split second, Johnny surged forward with an incredible amount of speed. With a warrior's yell, he sliced across Zeus's throat with the same golden knife he'd cut his palms with.

What the fuck was happening?

CHAPTER EIGHTEEN

Ivy

With wide, shocked eyes, Zeus dropped his lightning staff and brought his hands to his throat. Blood gushed through his fingers, and he dropped to his knees. Thunder rolled in the distance and the sky darkened as billowing black clouds spread across the sky.

"You fool!" Hera rushed to Zeus's side, dropping down beside him. "If he dies, we all die!"

"Mother! It's time for the only queen to rise to power! This is what you've always wanted! Finish him!" Johnny pulled out a whistle that was on a string around his neck and blew as hard as he could. "Our army will lead us to victory!"

My heartbeat pounded in my ears. Or was that the sound of wolves running through the forest?

Hera's eyes turned gold. "His lightning will destroy us all! How could you do this!"

Johnny grabbed Hera, moving her away from Zeus as hundreds of wolves came through the forest. The sleeping gas must have worn off, or reinforcements had arrived.

"You can stop them, Ivy. They are yours and you are theirs." Artemis ran after Johnny and Hera, leaving me with a gravely wounded Zeus right in the path of rabid wolves that wanted to rip our throats out.

What the hell did she mean they were mine?

I had only seconds before they were on top of us. My wolf took over, bursting free with the loudest snarl I'd ever produced. It traveled across the yard, dust flying up from the wolves as they got closer and closer.

Something innate told me to protect Zeus at all costs, and I leapt in front of him. But the wolves never came.

The dust slowly cleared, and they had all come to a stop, their glossy eyes locked on me. A gurgle came from next to me and then a hand clamped around my back ankle.

"You are their leader. You must make them heed to your command." Zeus's voice was faint in my mind.

"I'm not strong enough." There were at least two hundred wolves.

"You are. Reach for your power."

I found my power easily enough. Four strands of it, ebbing and flowing as they danced around each other. I grabbed on, using it as if it were my own.

"Shift."

At first nothing happened, but then it was like a wave of naked bodies took over the yard and surrounding forest. I whimpered as hundreds of connections suddenly formed. The noise knocked me back, and I threw all my defenses at blocking them from overwhelming me. There was so much pain and suffering in their confused words.

"Breathe, Ivy." Apollo was suddenly in front of me. "I need you to shift back and help me heal my father."

Shift back? What was he talking about?

"Ivy." Xander's gentle voice drew my attention to the left and to a pair of worried green eyes. *"Zeus needs you."*

Zeus?

Why the hell would Zeus need me? Awareness returned like a smack in the face and I shifted, the grass digging into my bare knees and the palms of my hands.

"Here." Xander pulled a shirt over my head, his naked chest the first thing I saw when my head emerged from the neck of it. "Cole is moving Silas and Eli to a safer location."

I looked around at the chaos surrounding us. Besides the wolves shifting back, the ones that had been passed out were starting to wake up.

My attention landed on Zeus, who was holding his throat as Apollo crouched next to him. "I need your help. I used too many of my resources earlier."

Apollo needed *my* help?

I scrambled over to them, dropping to my knees on the opposite side of Zeus. He stared up at me, his blue eyes now almost white as the color faded from them.

"On the count of three, we throw everything we have at him." Apollo took my hands in his and pressed them over Zeus's, covering his neck. "He would heal himself, but coming here takes a lot of energy for an old man like him."

Zeus made a gargling sounding growl and Apollo laughed. Did almost dying mean nothing to these people?

"Let's just do this." I was shaking like a leaf, but more from the adrenaline leaving my body.

Where had Johnny gone? Where was my mother?

"One, two, three."

A bright flash of light had me shutting my eyes as my hands tingled. This was different from healing Silas. It felt like energy was pouring in from all around me.

From my pack.

"We're done." Apollo let go of my hands and stood, offering Zeus his hand. "Sorry I was late for the fun. Had some wolves to save. Where's Art?"

I stared as Zeus was pulled to his feet, and the two gods zeroed in on the forest to the side of the house. They both took off, leaving me in their wake.

"Go." Xander put his hand on my cheek. "I can tell you want to. We'll still be here when you get back."

Fuck.

He was right, I did have this odd desire to go watch Zeus smite Johnny.

I was exhausted but used the last bit of energy to run after Apollo and Zeus... my uncle and grandfather.

I was about to laugh at the thought when a ball of fire flew past me.

Lightning cracked through the sky, hitting up ahead, and I went straight for it, knowing it could only be from one person. What I wasn't expecting was for there to be a ring of fire surrounding Artemis.

"I will kill her!" Johnny was covered head to toe in flames. He looked like something out of a movie.

I gasped, everyone's attention turning to me. I yanked the shirt I was wearing farther down, hoping I was covered enough. I didn't care so much anymore about nudity, but something about their stares made me want to shrivel up and hide.

"Perfect! Here she is now!" Every time Johnny spoke, flames shot out of his mouth. "Either Artemis or her. That's what I want."

"You aren't taking her!" Artemis tried to push her way out of the flames but fell back onto the ground. "Or me! Father, do something!"

Zeus's eyes were molten gold, and I shuddered. I had no clue what was going on or why Johnny was talking about taking me or Artemis, but Zeus didn't look happy about it.

"Hephaestus, you insolent child. You have a wife." Zeus sounded bored. "After trying to kill me, you really think you're going to get a second wife?"

Johnny threw another fireball at Zeus, who hit it with his staff like it was a fucking baseball. It crashed into a tree, causing it to burst into flames. They were going to burn the forest down if they didn't get Johnny under control.

"You did all of this because you wanted another wife?" I wished I could see the look on my own face. "But we're... related." I gagged.

"I hadn't entertained the idea of taking another wife, but now I demand it. I never got to choose my first." He was pacing back and forth, leaving a trail of fire everywhere he walked. "If my own mother doesn't appreciate me, I'll find someone and make them love me."

"You thought building an army of wolves was going to earn my love?" Hera was standing next to Zeus now, a bored expression on her face. Meanwhile, the forest was on fire and Artemis was still trapped. "My days of caring who Zeus slept with eons ago are in the past."

A scream ripped from Johnny's throat, fire spreading around us all. I screamed and scrambled closer to Apollo, who had a smirk on his face. He was enjoying this.

"That's enough." Zeus raised his staff in the air and the sky opened up, sending heavy rain down to put out the flames. "We'll deal with you back home." He pointed his staff at Johnny and a rope of lightning wrapped around him.

And just like that, it was over. How anticlimactic.

Hera came to me at the same time Artemis did. I could tell they didn't like each other by the stiffness in their spines as they brushed shoulders.

"Join us. We will teach you what you need to know about our world." Hera grabbed one of my hands.

I wanted to yank it away but gave it a small squeeze instead. "That's a hard pass for me."

Zeus came to join us, leaving his staff in Apollo's possession to keep the lightning wrapped around Johnny. "You can have everything you've ever imagined, but you'd rather stay here? In this... filth?"

His stare was penetrating, and I wondered if he'd changed his mind about me. They seemed to run by their own rules, which were heavily dependent on their emotions.

I put my hands on my hips and realized Artemis was doing the same thing. "This is my home. I'm a wolf, not a goddess."

"But you are. You need training and-" Apollo started to talk but Artemis turned and pinned him with a glare.

"You shall visit us." Zeus's voice held finality and I bit my tongue to stop myself from saying something back. "Artemis, I trust you will take care of your wolves?"

"Yes, father." She did a slight bow to him and then Zeus, Hera, Apollo, and Johnny were circled with blinding light and disappeared.

"What the hell?" A laugh burst out of me and then tears.

All the shit that had happened to us had been because a man couldn't handle his mother not giving him enough attention?

"It's been a few centuries since we've had to deal with Hephaestus's mommy issues." Artemis put her arm around me in an awkward hug. "I never imagined he'd stoop so low to use wolves in an attempt to overthrow my father."

"He didn't even care about you or me. My entire life was because you people just don't know how to communicate!" I pulled away from her, pissed off at the whole situation. "One star!"

"One star?" Artemis's eyebrows furrowed in confusion. "I actually have thousands of stars if you want more than one."

I threw my hands up and started walking back toward the house. We'd almost all died because of her and I just wanted to be with my mates.

"How about five stars? Would that make you happy?" Artemis caught up to me and grabbed my arm, pulling me to a stop. "You're angry? Did you want to be his wife?"

"Just... go home, Artemis." I pulled away from her. "You've done enough damage."

Turning my back to her, I walked toward the house. There were a lot of things that needed to be taken care of still. Hopefully, the coalition had captured everyone from OQ.

I was bone deep tired and my feet were practically dragging fifteen minutes later when I got to the house. Artemis was already there, hugging both wolves and people. She glowed faintly each time she touched them, and I stopped to watch, not sure what she was up to.

"She's giving them comfort." Xander stood from where he was sitting on the deck steps. "She said you wouldn't accept any stars, and this was the least she could do."

I sat down next to him. "Why aren't you inside?"

Cole, Eli, and Silas were nowhere to be seen, but I could sense them inside the house.

"I guess I'd hoped to see some of my old pack." He shrugged and wrapped an arm around my waist. "Trevor said Apollo was able to get all the other wolves out and stop any that were on trucks on their way here. They were planning on taking over our territory. Something about it being a prime location."

"I told Artemis to leave." I put my head on his shoulder. "All of this pain and suffering was because of some marital spat between Hera and Zeus. My entire life was determined based on an oath that wasn't even in play anymore."

"Without it, we wouldn't have all come together like we have. Surely that has to count for something." He stood and held out his hand. "Let's go see if our boy has come back to us."

Artemis met my stare from across the field and gave me a sad smile. I wanted a relationship with her, but what would that cost me? It was a decision for another day when my emotions weren't such a wreck.

I followed Xander into the house, hoping I'd finally be able to enjoy my new family and the new me.

CHAPTER NINETEEN

Eli

*W*armth surrounded me as I ran through the forest, the cool dirt under my paws. It had been a long time since I ran so freely without a care in the world. The smell of the trees and the clean air brought me new life, and I pushed myself harder, running faster than I ever had before.

I came to a beautiful house that I hadn't seen before. It was a chic log cabin style, with large stones and wood adorning the outside. A large terrace spread across the entire back of the house, providing a large patio area underneath.

The pond in the expansive yard reflected the lights shining from the floor-to-ceiling windows at the back of the house. Moving in closer, I was in awe of the wood and stonework. A lot of love went into building the house.

A woman's laugh came through the open sliding door and my ears perked up. Mate.

My mate? What in the hell?

I moved toward the house, marveling at how warm and inviting the inside looked through the windows with dark wood tones and creams. I wanted to curl up on the big rug in front of the fireplace.

The door was open into part of the living room and there she was. My mate, Ivy. I wasn't sure how I knew her name, but it flitted around in my mind, the sound of it making my tail wag.

Standing just outside the door, I observed her as she read a book. She laughed again, and this time a man came from around the corner and slid his arms around her, kissing her neck.

No one touched my mate. She was mine.

The book she held fell to the floor as she turned in her seat and began kissing him. His hands went to her hair and pulled it out of its bun, her thick red locks fanning out around her.

I lowered my head and growled, the man pulling away from her and cocking his head to the side while staring right at me.

Mate.

I backed up a step, surprised. A man? My mate too?

The man said something as he walked toward the door and then pulled it closed. Locking me out. Did he not see me?

I whimpered and put my nose against the glass, peering in at him lifting her out of her chair. Her legs wrapped around his waist as they kissed again. They walked out of the room without another glance my way.

I tilted my head back and howled.

"Eli?" Warm hands ran up and down my back as my eyes opened.

It was dark, and I felt like I was drifting on a cloud. My eyes shut again, wanting to drift off back to sleep. I wanted to see Ivy again, even if that meant standing outside all night.

"Baby, you're back." Xander's lips trailed across my shoulder to my neck. "Open those beautiful brown eyes."

Xander.

My eyes opened wide, and I scrambled up and out of the bed. At first, I didn't recognize where I was, but then everything came crashing down on me. *Holy shit.*

I looked down at my body, examining it before rushing to the bathroom and looking in the mirror. Everything appeared normal besides my scruffy appearance complete with overgrown facial hair.

Turning on the sink, I grabbed my toothbrush and started brushing vigorously. All I could taste was bile and dirt. I had no clue what had even happened. One second we were coming in from outside, and the next, nothing. Absolutely nothing. Maybe that was for the best, though.

The shower turned on, and I looked at Xander in the mirror. It seemed like it had been so long since I'd been awake and I didn't want to take my eyes off of him.

I grabbed the electric razor and turned it on. I hated

the feel of a lot of hair on my face and wanted it gone pronto.

"Where's Ivy?" My voice was hoarse as I started shaving off the beard that was starting to grow. I didn't know how Cole and Silas could stand it.

"They went to the store." He came toward me. "Do you um..." He looked at the bathroom door and then back at me, uncertainty in his eyes.

I handed him the shaver, not sure why it was so damn awkward between us. Had I bitten someone again? Been out of it for a month? Two months? My hair wasn't too long so it couldn't have been longer than that.

Shutting my eyes, I let him shave my face, making a mess all over the counter and floor, but I didn't care. "How long have I been out of it?"

Xander inhaled sharply and paused his shaving. "Two weeks. Not even Artemis could snap you out of it. You at least started letting us sleep near you. We thought maybe you weren't going to come back from it, and we'd have to get you a leash to take you on walks."

I snorted back a laugh as he started to shave above my lip. Two weeks was a long time to be stuck in wolf form, but I hadn't exactly been honest with myself and how everything was affecting me.

Ripping out Silas's neck still haunted me. Not to mention the fear I'd had at knowing they had my sister. Imagining any of the other wolves being with them even longer made me shudder.

Xander clicked off the shaver, putting it on the counter. He cupped my cheek and moved his thumb across the now smooth skin. "Where'd you go just now?"

"What?" I put my hand over his, needing his touch to ground me.

"When you're thinking too much, your eyes go glossy, and you stare off into space." His hand moved down to my jaw and his thumb moved across my lips. "We're safe now."

"Are we?" I walked to the shower and got in. I just needed to wash the last two weeks away. If that was even possible. "Because I thought after Dante we were safe and look what happened."

The warm water hit my skin and I groaned, every nerve ending firing with sensation. I stood there for several minutes before grabbing my loofah and squirting my body wash onto it.

"Why are we down here in my old room?" I asked Xander, who was leaning against the entrance of the shower watching me.

"We thought being somewhere familiar like your own room would help." His eyes tracked my movements as I started cleaning myself. "I should go call them and let them know you're back."

"You aren't going to help me wash my back?" We both knew I could wash my own back. "Join me."

"I don't think that now's the time for-" I shut him up by grabbing his shirt and yanking him in with me. "Eli-"

My lips crashed into his, not caring if I was getting his clothes wet. I needed to know that everything was okay and being with him was the only way I knew how.

We broke apart for a second so he could take off his shirt and then our lips were back on each other again, our tongues colliding and hands starting to roam as the rest of his clothes fell with a smack on the shower floor.

He snatched the loofah from me and spun me around, pushing me against the shower wall. "I believe you wanted your back washed."

I groaned as he washed my back while rubbing the head of his cock between my ass cheeks. I wanted him so bad my balls were aching.

Somehow, I managed to finish my shower and we stumbled, wet bodies and all, into the dim bedroom. The bed was a disaster with tangled sheets, dirt, and hair. I didn't want my dick touching any of that.

Maybe he was right and it wasn't the time.

"Come here." He grabbed a bottle of lube from the nightstand and pulled me toward my desk. "Get me ready." Pushing papers out of the way, he laid his chest across my desk, his ass pointing straight toward me, and his hands spreading his cheeks.

"Fuck, Xan." I snatched the bottle from where he'd set it down and squirted it down his crack. "You're so fucking perfect."

He hummed his approval as I teased his hole with my finger before slowly pushing it in. I damn near detonated just from how he squeezed my finger as I worked it in and out.

"More. I'm not going to break." He pushed his ass back as I added a second one. "Yes, fuck. Just like that, baby. God, I've missed you."

"You missed my cock?" I added a third, hitting him just right to make him arch his back. "Did you let anyone else fuck this ass while I was gone?"

He groaned, his breaths shortening as I pulled my fingers out and lined up with his entrance. "No. Only for you."

"That's right." I ran my hand down his spine. "Mine."

I pushed into him, both of us gasping as I filled him. He was so hot and tight, I was going to explode after a few thrusts if I didn't go slow.

"Fuck me hard. Make me yours again." Xander looked back over his shoulder. "Claim me."

So much for slow.

I grabbed his hips as I pulled out so just the tip was in him. "I claim you my way." I slowly pushed in, my entire body trembling, holding myself back. "You've always been mine."

"Elias." His voice was strained, and his hands gripped the back edge of the desk as I pulled out again. "Fuck me into this damn desk or I swear I'll—fuck yes!"

I slammed back into him, giving him what he wanted. Our skin slapped together with each snap of my hips, the desk jolting each time I thrust home.

He let go of his death grip on the desk and stroked his cock, making the most erotic sounds I'd ever heard each time I hit his prostate. My entire body tensed for a split second and then snapped with my last thrust into him.

"Xander!" My shout was loud; if someone was hanging around outside, they would have heard it.

He squeezed me as I came, his own cry of pleasure sending tingles to every single part of my body. I collapsed onto him, our bodies heaving from exertion.

"I can't feel my feet." Xander rested his cheek against the desk. "I think I broke my dick with how hard I was going at it."

Kissing his shoulder, I slowly pulled out, grabbing some tissues from the other side of the desk to clean us both up. We'd definitely need to have a second shower.

"I'm never going to get any work done at this desk now. Every time I sit here, I'll think about this." I gave his ass a smack and then smoothed my hand over the tight globe. "Please tell me there's food and that the grocery trip everyone is on isn't because there is none."

"There's groceries. We're having a cookout for Silas's birthday. Plus, we've been buying food for the last of the wolves that stuck around. They didn't eat much at first, but now they eat enough to even make Cole go broke." Xander groaned as he peeled himself from the desk. "Most of the wolves in that missing wolf database were found."

"And your pack?" I watched as his face fell. "None of them?"

"Some of them." He started to walk past me, and I stopped him. "I just want to move on, all right? There's no point in thinking about all the things that could have happened to them. No one remembers when the last time they saw them, so I'm just going to assume the worst."

Maybe one day we'd find out the specifics of what happened to his friends. I let him go, knowing that the best thing for all of us to do was try to move on with our lives even though it hurt.

CHAPTER TWENTY

Silas

"Listen, I'm not saying it has to be tonight." My laugh was obnoxious as Ivy shoved me down the personal care aisle. When we had walked past it, I'd made sure to drag her down it and head straight for the lube.

I was lucky she enjoyed my playful prods toward prodding her ass with my dick, otherwise I'd be sleeping on the couch or out in the doghouse.

"It's going to be never." She huffed as she tried to shove me further, but my feet were firmly planted in place. "And we have enough lube, don't we?"

"You can never have too much. I thought maybe you might want to try a different kind." I grinned as she rolled her eyes and started to walk away. "Oh, come on."

"It's a good thing you're cute." She purposely swung her hips as she walked, teasing me. "Maybe Cole will be up for it. You two hold hands and cuddle. It wouldn't be that big of a leap."

"What's not that big of a leap?" Cole stopped at the end of the aisle, the full cart of groceries ready to go to check out. His eyes went to the sign above the aisle. "We have lube."

"He wants what he always wants." Ivy looped her arm through Cole's and looked over at me. "My ass."

Cole grinned. "Come on, it's the boy's birthday. Give him what he wants."

"What he wants is a punch to the nut sack."

They laughed as I covered my crotch. It was small moments like these that made me forget everything that had completely gone to shit in our lives.

It had been a tough decision to come to the store and leave Eli, but now that we were here, it was a much needed break from our reality. A reality that left me feeling sick to my stomach most of the time.

After the OQ was taken down along with their psychotic leader, we had hoped to find a new normal again, but we'd been in a constant state of worry over Eli. No matter what we did, we couldn't get him to come back to us.

Maybe we had never mattered much to him in the first place.

"Hey, stop that." Cole let Ivy push the cart and fell back to walk beside me.

"Stop what? She said she thought my persistence was cute." I gave him a smile that felt fake as hell.

"Having morbid thoughts. I can see it written all over your face." He snagged me around my neck with his arm and pulled me toward him. "He'll snap out of it eventually."

"It's been two weeks." I started losing hope he'd come back to us when he let Xander and Ivy snuggle up to him the night before.

He wasn't snapping and growling at us now, and I thought it was a bad idea to let him get comfortable in that way. Why come back when it was easier to just block everyone and everything out?

"He'll come back when he's ready. He's just not ready yet." Cole gave me a squeeze and then moved to the conveyor belt to help unload the cart.

It felt wrong to be celebrating my birthday when everything was a mess. The coalition had caught most of the people behind OQ, but part of me still didn't believe it could be over so easily. It was almost like a sick joke that someone was playing on us.

It was highly unlikely that only the OQ knew about our existence and that scared the crap out of me. Anytime someone even looked at me now, I wondered if they were assessing me.

"Looks like someone's birthday is soon!" The woman scanning the groceries smiled warmly at us as she moved my birthday cake to the bagging area. "How old is your son turning?"

"Thirty-five." Ivy looked at me with a smile. "It was the only one you guys had that was Funfetti."

I happened to think the dinosaur design was

awesome. Why couldn't a grown ass man enjoy a cake with a *Tyrannosaurus rex* printed on it?

∽

ONCE WE WERE BACK HOME, Cole popped the trunk of the SUV and we loaded our arms up with bags. Ivy grabbed the cake and rolled her eyes as I added another bag to my arm.

"You guys could take two trips, you know." Ivy held open the door leading into the house, my cake balanced in one hand.

I hadn't even wanted a celebration, but we were keeping things simple with just close friends and family. It seemed ridiculous to celebrate without Eli, but Ivy had been persistent.

"But why would we do that when we can carry them in one trip?" I shimmied through the doorway sideways since my arms were loaded with bags.

"In our new house, we're going to install a zip line and just send them flying to the kitchen." Cole grunted as he adjusted the weight of his bags. "It'll be easier to carry in all the gallon containers of lube too."

"We are not going to install a zip line for our lube." Eli stood at the end of the hall, looking like he hadn't just been stuck in his wolf. His hair was slicked back and his face freshly shaved.

I came to a screeching halt, Cole bumping into me and sending a few bags every which way. I didn't care. I dropped my entire load and barreled down the hall.

Eli opened his arms for me, and I crashed into him,

nearly taking us both to the floor. I wanted to laugh and cry but settled on burying my face in his shirt. I was so fucking gone for all of them.

"I couldn't miss your birthday." He patted my back awkwardly. "You can let go now."

"I'm never letting you go." I made a gagging noise. "Fuck, see what you assholes have done to me? I used to be this big, bad biker dude and now I'm just..."

I backed away, my face heated, realizing everyone was watching me. *Damn it.*

"You only wished you were a badass." Cole grabbed Eli and pulled him into a hug. "We missed you."

Ivy was still standing at the door, my cake in her hands. Stepping over the groceries we'd left in the hall, I took it from her. "Go on, bunny. Don't be shy."

She was trembling, and I resisted the urge to throw the cake down and take her in my arms. She'd been our rock over the last few weeks when it should have been the other way around. We'd been a mess and she was the glue that held us together.

With tears already threatening to spill over, she and Eli moved toward each other. Eli took her hands and brought them to his lips.

"I'm sorry," he whispered.

She flung herself at him, bursting into tears. Hell, tears were even streaming down my cheeks. He picked her up, her legs wrapping around him, and he carried her to his bedroom without another word from either of them.

"Let's get these groceries put away." Xander came up

behind me and put his hand on my shoulder. "I would have called you guys but didn't want you to rush."

I snorted and headed for the kitchen with my cake. "Bullshit. You just wanted to fuck him."

Xander held his hands up in mock surrender. "Well, actually he did the fucking. He seems to be quite randy at the moment."

"You can say that again." Cole followed with at least ten grocery bags. He was such a showoff. "Ivy isn't exactly being quiet."

I adjusted myself, resisting the urge to go in there and join in. There wouldn't be a problem with that, but at the same time, if it were me just coming back from being stuck in my wolf, I'd want to be alone with my girl.

"Should we cancel the party? I don't want Eli to feel overwhelmed." It wasn't going to be a huge gathering, but still. "I don't need a party. I'll take a birthday dance though."

Xander was staring at the cake I just put on the counter. "I don't give lap dances for free. I have to earn money somehow and little boys don't have a lot of money."

"Oh, I'll show you little boy." I grabbed my crotch as laughter filled the kitchen.

We continued to banter back and forth as we put the groceries away. The only thing I wanted was them: my family.

CHAPTER TWENTY-ONE

Xander

Things were finally starting to look up for us. Eli was back, our pack was healing, and the coalition was getting the other wolves the help they needed to get back to their lives. I just wished wherever my friends ended up, they were at peace.

Now that I wasn't looking over my shoulder every two minutes, I could focus on figuring out what I wanted to do with the rest of my life. Running the pack with Ivy was not my thing, but it wasn't like I could go back to stripping.

Or could I?

"What are you up to?" Ivy came from behind me, slipping her arms around my neck. We'd all slept in after staying up far too late drinking and celebrating Silas's birthday the night before.

"Trying to figure out how to spend all this time I have." I clicked on a job posting for a delivery driver. "I like driving."

"Hm." She put her chin on the top of my head. "You don't need a job."

I put my tablet down and relaxed against the couch cushions as her hands scraped over my pecs. "I need to do something."

"Well... you could strip." She jumped over the back of the couch and landed next to me. "Or offer classes."

"Male stripping classes?" I pulled her into my lap, wrapping my arms around her. If I could spend all day cuddling with her or the others, that could be my job. "Maybe that place we took a dance lesson at is hiring."

"There you go." She brushed her lips over mine. "Everyone else is working from home. We can figure out something. Silas always complains about having to sell his stuff and ship it. Maybe you can be his bitch."

"If he wasn't nitpicky about the way things were bubble wrapped, then I'd be down with that. I really need something of my own to do." I'd never really put a lot of thought into a career, going straight from high school to stripping and then to being a beta.

Not that being a beta lasted long.

"You could help build the new house. I plan on helping a bit... hammer some nails, grout some tiles or something." Ivy laughed when I raised an eyebrow. "Hey, I know how to use a drill."

"Do you?" I threw my head back and laughed. When she'd tried to use the drill when we built Silas's studio, she'd squealed when the screw went in really fast.

"How can I get better at screwing if I don't practice?" She flinched, realizing what she'd just said. "That's not what I meant."

"Sure it's not." I kissed her, pulling her even closer. "Maybe that can be a job. Helping women learn to screw better."

"The only woman you're helping is me." She straddled me, wrapping her arms around my neck. "Can you teach me?"

"That can be arranged." I kissed across her collarbone and up her neck. "What are you willing to pay me?"

"Do you have a coupon?" She gasped as I bit her neck. "Do I get the friends and family discount?"

"You're asking for it." I lifted her and threw her on the couch, her tits bouncing. It should be illegal to unleash those. "Fuck, Ivy."

I moved on top of her, fitting perfectly between her legs. She arched up into me, her leg brushing against my quickly growing erection.

"Do the lessons come with unlimited make out sessions?" She started to lift the hem of my shirt.

"Really? Didn't you get enough last night?" Cole said from above us.

"Never enough." Ivy pulled my shirt off, throwing it right in Cole's face. "Just for that, none for you."

"None for Xander either. Let's go." Cole threw my shirt back at me, and I groaned. I'd forgotten we were working on something on the new property.

"I forgot." I jumped up, pulling my shirt on. I leaned

down and kissed Ivy's cheek. "Sorry, sweetie. Rain check?"

"I'll just take my business elsewhere then." She sat up and adjusted her shirt. "Where are you guys going?"

"To do things." Cole straightened the pillows on the couch. "No, you can't come."

"What kinds of things?" She smiled as she grabbed a pillow and messed it up.

The look on Cole's face was priceless. He looked at her, the pillow, then back at her, while putting his hands on his hips. I couldn't believe she'd do it in front of him either.

"Did you just do that on purpose?" His eyes narrowed even more, and he pointed a finger at her. "You've been doing it for weeks! Unfolding all the towels and putting them back wrong, leaving a knife every day with butter on it in the sink even though we ate nothing with butter. And the socks! Who unfolds a perfect trifold and makes a ball with them?"

"Why would she do that, man?" I was trying hard not to laugh because I knew exactly what Ivy had been doing to see his reaction. We'd all needed a laugh, and it certainly made Silas and me crack up.

"I don't know what you're talking about." She stood and made sure to move on the opposite side of me. It was great being a buffer between two pit bulls.

He gasped. "You're the one that opened all the chip bags from the wrong end and put all of the boxes in the pantry upside down!"

"Maybe we have a ghost." She darted around the couch, squealing as Cole took off after her.

I sat back, laughing as they played cat and mouse before Cole finally caught her—she totally let him—and rubbed his stubble against her neck. She squealed and squirmed to get away from him.

"You must want a good spanking." Cole bent her over the arm of the couch and her giggling abruptly changed to something halfway between a growl and a moan. "But, we have to go."

"Seriously?" She grabbed a pillow and whacked him with it. "If I find out you four are doing some kind of choo choo train, I'm not going to be happy."

"What do you mean?" I stood and stretched, looking around for my shoes.

"It's a train of you guys fucking each other. The question is, who is the caboose and doesn't get a dick in their-"

"Okay, I think we need to go before we devolve into thirteen-year-olds." Cole headed for the front door.

"What's wrong Coley-poo? Don't like to hear about a dick in your ass?" Ivy jumped out of his grasp. A new playful side of her was quickly emerging with each passing day. "I guess I better work on answering messages from the other packs."

"I don't miss that at all." He kissed her and passed her off to me. "I'll meet you in the truck."

"We're going to be gone until dinner." I put my forehead against hers. "I can't wait to watch him spank you later."

She swatted at me and I danced away, laughing.

There was no better feeling in the world than laughing with the people you loved.

CHAPTER TWENTY-TWO

Cole

We'd been working on the treehouse for a week, and it still wasn't perfect. We'd jokingly talked about rebuilding a treehouse in the past, but the more I thought about it, the more I needed it to happen.

Keeping it a secret from Ivy had been nearly impossible because she knew we were up to something when we kept disappearing. Lucky for us, she was busy training with Artemis and taking care of alpha business.

"It's missing something." I stood back and looked up at it. "It's too plain."

"It's a treehouse." Silas lifted his shirt and wiped his brow. "What else could it possibly need besides a few windows and a ladder?"

Xander came to stand next to me, rubbing his chin as he looked upward. "I think he's right. It just kind of stands out up there in the trees. If we want to fuck up there without being disturbed, it needs to be camouflaged."

"Pretty sure if we're fucking up there, someone down here will hear us." Eli started to clean up the tools we had out everywhere. "Maybe we can paint it to blend in with the trees."

"I think it needs some vines or something natural." Silas climbed up the ladder. "Maybe we can let Ivy decorate it."

I climbed halfway up, grabbing one of the thick folding mattresses from Xander and handing it up to Silas. "Is there going to be enough space for all of these?"

When Silas didn't take the second one, I climbed up and stuck my head through the door. Where the fuck was he?

"Silas?" I climbed all the way up. "What the fuck?"

I spun around in a circle and went to the window, peering out. Had he jumped?

"Cole." His voice was muffled, and I turned to look around the empty room. The only thing inside was what we'd already carried up. "I'm right here."

My eyes landed on the large branch coming through the floor and out the side of the wall. I squinted, not sure I was seeing correctly.

"Silas?" I stepped forward but stumbled back when two knots in the branch opened and blue eyes stared back at me. "Holy fuck. You're... what... how? Eli! Xander!"

"Get down from there! The whole top of the tree is shaking!" Eli yelled up to us.

"I'm stuck." Silas was laughing hysterically. "It just sucked me in and now I can't get out!"

Words failed me, and I just stared open-mouthed at the two eyes staring back at me. How the hell did that even happen in the first place? Did it open up and eat him? Or maybe a branch grabbed him and then he melted into the branch.

"Stay calm." His eyes blinked, bark covering them each time. "Go find Artemis." When I didn't move, the treehouse shook. "Go!"

I scrambled down the ladder, my heart racing. "Silas! He's the tree!" I grabbed Eli's shoulders and shook him. "The fucking tree!"

Eli looked at me like I was crazy and looked up at the treehouse. "What?"

"He's the tree!" I went over to the trunk and smacked my hand on it.

"Ow! Fucker, that hurt!" Silas's voice was distorted in the way one would expect; deep and booming.

I was never going to be able to touch a tree again. What if it was one of his kind and could feel everything? Oh my God, how many tree people had I killed in my life?

Not panicking in the slightest, Xander came over next to me and ran his hand seductively up the side of the tree. "Do you think when he gets an erection a new branch pops out?"

"Fuck you, man." The tree shook, leaves floating down to the ground.

Xander laughed, his amusement contagious. "Actually, it would probably be a twig."

"Someone go get Artemis so I can get out of here and kick his-" He stopped talking suddenly, and then his head appeared from around the tree trunk. "Never mind. Figured it out."

"Too late. I already told Ivy we had a tree emergency." Eli moved carefully toward Silas. "Are you all right?"

"I'm fine. I feel like I had a quadruple shot of espresso." He finally moved out from behind the trunk butt ass naked and as hard as the tree he just came from. "And I'm horny as hell."

"Or are you thorny?" Xander smirked.

"You better watch it, or I'll fuck your ass right here against my tree." Silas stroked the bark like it was a pet. "My seed needs to be spread."

"Is that a threat or a promise?"

"It's a-"

"What's going on here?" Ivy had appeared out of nowhere, Artemis right behind her. They both moved so fast that if you weren't watching or blinking, it appeared like they came from nowhere.

At least now we knew that Apollo wasn't just appearing out of thin air when he showed up. We were still nervous he'd come back to bother us again, but Artemis assured us the thumb war had been won fair and square.

Ivy's eyes went straight to the treehouse and her

face lit up. "You built a treehouse? Why didn't you tell me? I could have used my drill!" She skipped to the ladder, her excitement making my own build.

Silas grabbed her elbow, steering her away. "Not so fast, bunny."

Her eyes fell to his dick. "Why are you naked?"

"He's claimed this tree." Artemis stood near the trunk, almost with her nose against it. "A good, solid first choice."

"Claimed it, as in he..." Ivy stared wide-eyed at Silas. "Did you fuck a hole or something pervy like that?"

"No." Silas moved Ivy in front of him as he turned to talk to Artemis. "But how did I claim it?"

It was too weird for any of us to be naked in front of our mate's mother. Plus, she wasn't a wolf.

"Well, what were you thinking about when it pulled you in?" Artemis walked around the trunk of the tree and bent down to pick something up. "It takes a minute, but the tree usually gives you your clothes back."

They were perfectly folded, his boots sitting neatly on top of the stack. I rubbed my eyes and wondered if the mushrooms in the omelet from breakfast were psychedelic.

"I don't know. I guess I was thinking about how perfect the trees were that we picked." Silas took the clothes from Artemis and stayed behind Ivy as he pulled his pants back on. "I touched it."

"Your mind and heart were open to accepting the tree into your life and the tree felt the same desire."

Artemis clapped her hand together. "Ivy will become even more powerful now."

"I think I'm powerful enough. No need for any superhero powers." Ivy walked to the ladder again. "Can I see inside?"

"We were going to set it up and surprise you." I crossed my arms. "But if you really can't wait..."

She looked over her shoulder at me and gave me a saucy smile. "Artemis was just about to leave."

"Was I?" She looked around at each of us. "Oh, yes, I get it!"

Artemis vanished, dust flying in her wake.

"Let's take this baby for a ride." Ivy climbed up the ladder, none of us moving to follow her because we were watching her.

"The only reason Cole wanted to rebuild the treehouse was to stand here and watch that." Silas made an appreciative sound in his throat.

"You heard the woman." Xander grabbed the last folding mattresses and scurried up the ladder.

Eli went up after him leaving me and Silas. He was staring up at the tree, uncertainty written all over his face.

"I can just stay down here and listen." He set his shirt on the ground and plopped down. "Make sure to swivel your hips in that way she likes so I can hear her screams down here."

My dick perked at that, and I went to the ladder. "Just don't think about the tree. You got yourself out of it once."

"I'd rather not risk it. What if I'm in the middle of

fucking our girl and turn to wood? She'll be screaming for a different reason." He shuddered.

"I doubt you'd give her splinters." I ran up the ladder as he threw his boot at me.

Xander and Eli already had Ivy completely naked by the time I got into the treehouse. Her rosy nipples were hard, and her perfect pussy was waiting to be claimed.

"Is this the only reason you guys built this?" Ivy shut her eyes as Xander knelt in front of her and lifted her leg to put over his shoulder. She leaned back against Eli, who was pinching her nipples. "Not that I'm complaining."

I stalked closer, my eyes locked on hers. "We rebuilt it because we love you."

Grasping her chin, I took her lips in a gentle kiss and captured her moans as Xander and Eli got her ready for all of us.

It hadn't always been easy, but building a life with her was everything I never knew I needed.

CHAPTER TWENTY-THREE

Ivy

These men were my everything. All of my doubts had disappeared a long time ago, and now it was just me and them, ready to take on anything that was thrown at us.

Including Silas becoming one with the tree.

"Where's Silas?" My entire body was thrumming with anticipation as Xander moved his fingers inside me and teased my clit with his tongue.

"Scared." Cole backed away from us and pulled his shirt off.

His body was a work of art, and my wolf staring back at me from the center of his chest made tears well in my eyes. I'd seen them all with them, but right then, it hit me that these men would do anything for me.

"Sweetheart." Eli kissed my neck and turned my face to him. "Why are you crying?"

"I'm not." I sniffled and then moaned as Xander did something with his tongue that made my core clench. "Just a little emotional."

"Right now is about you. Don't think about anything else." Eli kissed me softly and rolled my nipples between his fingers.

I gasped into his mouth as Xander's fingers fucked me into oblivion. My body was always so responsive to them, especially when we were all together. It was like my pussy knew more than one cock wanted to be inside.

Eli's mouth moved to my ear, my attention landing back on Cole, who had sat down against the wall and was stroking himself. "Do you want him to watch as Xander and I fuck you?"

"Yes." My legs trembled as my orgasm built. I knew exactly what Xander was prepping me for, and I clenched around his fingers. "I need both of you inside me."

Silas's head popped through the floor, his eyes landing right on Xander buried between my legs. He watched for a few breaths before his blue eyes lifted and found mine. "I wasn't hearing any screaming, so I thought I'd come investigate."

He hesitated before he slowly climbed up, remaining by the hatch he'd come through. I couldn't say I blamed him for not wanting to move farther in.

Xander hummed against my clit and then sucked and flicked it. I nearly buckled in half as my orgasm spiraled through me, sending a flood of heat and wetness between my legs. He grinned up at me, licking his lips, and lay back on the mattress.

"Come sit on my cock." Xander stroked himself, his eyes darkened with desire.

My legs were already feeling like noodles as I dropped to my knees and crawled over to him, giving Eli a view of my ass. He smacked it as I crawled on top of Xander, sending my desire back into high gear.

Lowering onto Xander, I tried to contain my excitement at the thought of both of them filling me. It made me so full and hit everywhere I needed every single time.

"This is killing me." Silas finally moved farther in, standing to take off his pants. "If I turn into a tree, I'm sorry."

"Stop thinking about it and you won't." Cole had his head back against the wall, his hand moving in long strokes as he watched Silas undress. "Although, is that a leaf?"

Silas looked at his dick frantically, the erection he'd had starting to soften. I was just about to tell Cole he was an ass when Eli moved behind me and pressed the tip of his cock against my entrance.

I leaned forward, giving him easier access to slide in alongside Xander, stretching me to my max. Whatever Xander had done with his fingers had helped me adjust quickly, and both of them began moving like they were one and the same.

"Oh, fuck." My fingers dug into the mattress as they fell into a rhythm that made my head spin.

Eli held onto my hips, stopping me from moving so they could both stay sheathed inside me. "Look at how turned on you've made Silas and Cole."

I had forgotten that Silas had thought his dick was growing a leaf. I glanced up, and my walls constricted, squeezing Xander and Eli. Cole had stood from where he'd been on the floor and both men were chest to chest, hands wrapped around each other's dicks.

"Deer on a cracker, that is the hottest fucking thing... oh, God. Yes." Someone's fingers were rubbing my clit. "I'm going to come."

Their pace increased, the sounds of our bodies coming together sending me over the edge. They pulled out before they could finish, leaving me whimpering from the loss of them.

Cole and Silas took their place, lifting me from the ground. I wrapped my legs around Silas and sank onto his cock. He took my mouth, our tongues tangling together as he walked forward before my back was against Cole's chest.

"Are you ready to be fucked by your alphas?" Cole bit my ear before he pushed inside.

We were in a precarious position—Cole's legs bent slightly as he leaned against one of the walls—and the angle and the added feeling of floating made me that much more ready for the two of them.

Xander had Eli on his hands and knees facing us, both of them watching. My nails dug into Silas's shoulders as they moved me on their cocks.

"Oh, yes. Right there," Eli panted as Xander took him from behind. The sounds of their skin smacking together was loud in the empty treehouse and only sped up my spiral toward another orgasm.

"Look at what you do to all of us, Alpha." Cole's teeth scraped down my neck, his fingers digging into my hips. "All of us fucking lost on how sexy you are."

Silas's eyes were locked on the connection between us, his dick sliding in and out of me. "You're ours. Forever."

"Yes!" Everything seized up as they hit me everywhere all at once.

"Bunny, fuck!" Silas took a nipple between his teeth, my orgasm intensifying as they both thrust one final time and exploded inside me.

Xander and Eli were already collapsed on the mattress. Xander was wrapped around Eli and stroking his arm. With my head still spinning, Cole and Silas lay me down in front of Eli.

With a satisfied sigh, I snuggled into Eli's chest, Silas moving behind me and wrapping his arm around my waist. There was nothing better than sweaty cuddling after multiple orgasms in our brand-new treehouse.

The sun was setting by the time we climbed down, and I walked out from the cover of the trees, looking across the pond to where our house would be built.

I'd moved to Arbor Falls because all I had wanted was to find myself. Instead, I found so much more.

I was home.

The End

Printed in Great Britain
by Amazon